TABBY MONROE

Howl FM

BLACK CHERRY
PUBLISHING

Contents

Keep in touch with Tabby!

Want to hear about Tabby's latest releases as they come out? Want exclusive sneak peeks, cover reveals, giveaways and other awesome stuff?

Hell yeah you do! Sign up for Tabby's newsletter here: https://www.tabbymonroe.com/newsletter/

Chapter 1

*T*he front door was shattered. It hung crooked on its hinges, its wood splintered and warped, and the paint gouged away in huge strips. Bree Mendez stared from the sidewalk, clenching her backpack strap in one hand and her bike helmet in the other. Cars rumbled along the street behind her, the sleepy morning traffic oblivious to the wreckage on the side of the road.

"Shit."

She nudged a shard of glass with the toe of her boot. It crackled across the paving stone. Broken glass littered the sidewalk, glittering in the crisp morning light, and the front of the Silver Bullet bar loomed in front of her, its windows punched in like a boxer's teeth.

"Shit," Bree said again. It bore repeating.

If this was a horror movie—one of the ones she watched most weekends, crammed on her sofa with the girls—she'd push the door open and walk inside. It'd be dark, too, and the door would creak on its hinges, and she'd call out for intruders as she walked blindly into the shadowed bar.

Screw that. Even first thing in the morning, Bree wasn't that dumb. She dug out her phone and called 911.

Boiling River may have been a small town, but the emergency lines were kept busy. It was natural, when the town was home to one of the biggest populations of supernatural creatures in the country.

Tempers ran high in the heat. Instincts were not always tamed. Accidents happened. And the tourists freaking loved that shit, poring over news articles and hoping for a mauling.

Bree was not a tourist. She just wanted to start her shift.

"Yeah, hi." The phone operator barked out questions as Bree relayed the scene. Yes, she worked here. No, she hadn't gone inside. No, she had no idea what happened. She eyed the building as they talked, wincing at the lines gouged into the front door and the shadows of wrecked furniture inside.

"Are valuables kept in the bar overnight?" The operator said everything in the same loud, clipped tone, like a drill sergeant giving commands. Bree grit her teeth, tamping down the urge to snipe back. She was reporting a crime, not screwing around.

"No." Besides cash, the only things worth a dime in the Silver Bullet were the retro jukebox and the speaker system. "Charlton takes the lock box home with him every night."

"That's not safe." Triumph rang down the phone line, like he'd caught Bree being careless. She rolled her eyes up at the gutters. As if she held any sway over her cranky old boss.

"He also takes a loaded shotgun."

The operator spluttered. "That's not safe either!"

... Alright. Bree was not a morning person, and this guy had reached the end of her rope. She squeezed the phone in her hand, forcing cheeriness into her voice as she kicked at the glass again.

"Cool, well, you should probably send someone over! Thanks for your help."

"Wait, hang on miss—"

She jabbed the screen with her thumb. Life was too damn short.

The morning sun shone hot on the back of her neck, and Bree rolled her head in a circle. It was stiff, the muscles sore from falling asleep on her sofa watching true crime documentaries at 3am. When she'd woken up this morning, she'd still been wearing last night's work t-shirt, the smell of stale beer wafting up from the fabric.

Gods, she needed a reset.

Bree clicked her tongue. This was Boiling River. The cops could be three minutes or three hours. Glass crunched under her boots as she strode to the bar's outer wall, tossing her backpack and bike helmet down in a heap. Then Bree turned, leaned her back against the brick, and tipped her face up to the sun.

An aching back. An overslept alarm. A half-destroyed bar. It was just another day in Boiling River, the desert town that had tethered her since birth.

Bree gusted out a heavy breath, closed her eyes, and wished for something interesting to happen.

* * *

There were lots of reasons a building might get wrecked in Boiling River.

Drunken tourists.

A sinkhole.

The wrath of a local god.

"Werewolves," Bree's boss Charlton declared as soon as he arrived. He scowled at the front of his ruined bar, hands shoved deep in the pockets of his leather vest, his shoulders bunched by his ears. He was a grizzly, grumbling ex-biker who'd settled in the valley when his hog broke down in Boiling River back in the eighties. He told Bree once the cost of fixing his prized bike or buying a tumbledown cottage out here were about the same.

Bree believed it. A couple years back, she'd saved up enough to take off and backpack around the world for six months. She'd thought she had enough for a year, but turns out Boiling River was dirt cheap compared to the big, wide world.

Apparently most people didn't want to live in the ass-crack of nowhere with a bunch of fairy tale monsters.

"Maybe." Bree scuffed her boot on the sidewalk. It was always supernatural creatures who got blamed for the slightest crime. And though those claw marks on the door were pretty damning, she wasn't about to throw around accusations without proof. "Danny will tell us more."

Charlton snorted, his salt and pepper mustache fluttering.

"That boy? He's only just outta diapers."

Danny was two years older than Bree. She said nothing.

Once upon a time, Bree was known around town as a firecracker—quick to anger, with a temper flashing hot. These days, though, she was more listless than lively. Her spark had gone out. She still went through the motions, tossing back shots behind the bar and chasing out sloppy drinkers with a pool cue, but her heart wasn't in it.

She shrugged. "He's gone through all the training. Danny's a good cop." She spoke to the single cloud drifting across the desert sky, like a cotton ball caught in a stream.

Charlton grumbled something under his breath. It must have been bad for him to mumble. He was a grouchy old fool, and vicious when he wanted to be, but Bree knew him better than anyone. He gave her this job when she dropped out of college and came back to Boiling River. And when her family moved to the west coast without her, he rented Bree her shitbox apartment at a fair rate.

After all these years, Charlton was family. Just… the kind of family that started fights at Thanksgiving.

The police car pulled up to the curb, the windows wound down and the radio humming. The police handset crackled over the music, calling out codes and street locations.

"Hey, Danny," Bree called as the leopard shifter killed the engine. He unfolded himself from the car, all graceful long limbs. "You draw the short straw?"

"Yes, ma'am." Danny was always so damn formal on duty. He'd been the same way when Claire was attacked by her vamp boyfriend's stalker a few months back. All *Miss Ramsden* and *a moment of your time*—like they hadn't all known him as a teenager sneaking bottles away to party in the valley. "We got your call about a break in." He leveled her a look. "You could have stayed on the line."

Bree gave a sharp smile. "No, I couldn't."

"It's for your safety."

"And look! I survived."

They could have gone on for a while, bickering like old friends, but Charlton cleared his throat then spat on the sidewalk. He stepped up to Danny, barrel chest straining his vest, white hairs curling over the zipper.

"This is the wolves' doing. See those claw marks?"

Danny glanced over his shoulder and nodded once, short and sharp.

"I see them. Lots of creatures round here with claws." He raised an eyebrow at the old biker, as if to remind him that *he* was one of them.

"It's the wolves," Charlton repeated, stubborn. "They're always raising Hell in my bar. Breaking glasses and knocking down stools." Danny whipped out a pad, scribbling a note and waving for Charlton to keep talking. Bree rolled her eyes and pushed away from the wall, strolling closer to the front door as they talked. Get Charlton started on one of his rants and you'd have three more gray hairs by the time it ended.

There were four claw marks total. Gouged deep into the wood, they stretched from her head height down to her waist. Bree sucked on her teeth, raising a hand and mimicking the shape of the slash.

"Don't touch that," Danny called out, voice curt. What was it with lawmen barking at her today? "That's evidence."

"I'm not an idiot," she called back without turning around. "Can I touch the air, Officer Danny? Or is that evidence too?"

Charlton guffawed behind her, and that told her to ease off. If her boss found her funny, she was usually being an ass. Bree stepped away from the door, palms held up, then stuffed her hands in her pockets. She could play nice.

Craning her neck, Bree peered through the shattered windows. The inside looked even worse than the front door—floorboards pried up; the pool table knocked on its side. Broken glass glittered from the floor.

No way were they opening up today. Not even if they could start cleaning up right now. Bree was down a shift, and with it, in trouble with her bank. Again.

"You need me here?" she called, cutting over Danny. If she could go now, maybe she could swing a shift at Hex Mex...

"Afraid so." Danny really did look sorry, his brown eyes knowing. Like he could see the tiny numbers flashing through her brain, see the panic brewing in her gut. It made her itch. "I'll need to take a statement, and then it would be good to have you here for the walk through. To see if anything's out of place."

Bree scoffed. "The whole damn bar's out of place." But she stomped back to the wall and leaned there again.

With her head tipped back and her eyes closed, Charlton's rant faded to a low hum. Passing traffic rumbled along the street, the vibrations buzzing through the sidewalk, and the rays of sunshine soaked into her skin. It was almost nice, if she let herself forget why she was here. Almost restful...

"Good morning, sunshine." A deep voice jerked Bree awake. She leaped forward, staggering away from the wall where she'd been dozing. Danny and Charlton were still huddled together talking, further down the sidewalk now, and the lone cloud was gone from the sky.

"Never took you for a napper."

Gods damn it. She should have known. The second Charlton had said wolves, she should have known they'd call *him*.

Otis Pascale. The Boiling River alpha. And the bane of Bree's existence.

Chapter 2

⚭

*O*tis stood on the sunny sidewalk and beamed at the frazzled bartender.

Bree Mendez. Crimson-lipped viper of a woman. His heart squeezed in his chest.

"I wasn't napping." She sounded furious, her cheeks flushing red at the suggestion. Like he hadn't just caught her first-hand, propped up against the faded brick wall, her mouth drooping open and soft snores coming from her mouth.

"Sure you weren't." Otis grinned, watching her eyes boil with rage. He had that effect on her.

Seeing Bree was exactly the distraction he'd needed this morning. Since he woke up, everything had gone wrong. His phone charger died. His car ran out of gas, forcing him to jog four miles to work. And when he'd arrived, sweating in the desert heat, he realized he forgot the key to the radio station.

Didn't matter. She was in front of him, which made today a Good Day. Even if she loathed the sight of him. Even if this was a crime scene.

"What's going on, Mendez?" He eyed the wrecked building behind her. "You finally snap?"

She huffed, but his eyes snagged on the claw marks gouged into the front door. That wasn't good. Twenty feet down the sidewalk, the Silver Bullet owner was huddled with a local cop. They muttered together, the cop making notes, and Otis didn't need heightened senses to catch the word *werewolves.*

Shit. This wasn't his pack's work—no way. He raised those wolves right, damn it, and though he was laid back by nature, he kept them in line.

This? This was criminal damage. Otis and his pack had no part in it.

"Why am I here?" he asked Bree, trying to sound pleasant. It came out wrong, even to his own ears. He sounded pissed off.

The bartender threw up her hands, then scrubbed at her face.

"I don't know," she muttered between her fingers. "I mean, I *do* know. Charlton thinks your wolves did this."

Otis figured as much, but he was glad to hear her say it. At least she didn't say she thought the wolves were guilty. At least she had the guts to tell him the truth.

"They didn't say so on the phone."

Bree muttered something into her hands. Something like *freaking cowards.* It buoyed him, puffing his chest up again. Gods, she was beautiful. Her dark hair was tied back in a messy bun, and strands had escaped to fall around her shoulders. More than anything, Otis wanted to reach out and wind a lock of her hair around his knuckle. To feel the silky soft strands against his rough skin; to watch the chestnut highlights catch the sunshine.

"Don't worry," he told her instead. "I won't tell them about your famous temper." He said it loud enough to carry down the sidewalk; to make the cop look over, face curious. Bree punched his shoulder hard, her face flaming, making him snort and stagger back. "Careful," Otis warned. "There are witnesses. People might talk."

"You piece of..." Bree broke off, strangling the air before massaging her temples. "I don't have claws," she muttered after a moment, dropping her hands. "Unlike some people, I couldn't have done this."

She was right. Otis sobered, sliding his phone out of his back pocket and shooting off a message to the pack group chat. He needed everyone's alibis for last night. He wanted everyone accounted for.

It didn't matter that he'd lived here for over ten years. Didn't matter that in all that time, Otis hadn't gotten so much as a parking ticket. He was the leader of the pack, which meant he was responsible. If one of his had done this, he'd go down for it too. And if Otis had a weakness, it was collecting waifs and strays. Anyone who needed somewhere to belong, he let in.

They didn't even have to be werewolves, truly. He ran Supernatural Airwaves like a pack all of its own. A pack of misfits and vampires and shifters and ghosts, and a cupid thrown in for good measure.

No. It didn't matter that Otis had never missed a town meeting. That he coached the high school track team. There was no such thing as a respectable werewolf, even in Boiling River. People were people, and people got scared of anybody different.

Even brave people like Bree.

* * *

The cop had the grace to look uncomfortable as Otis strode over. He walked with his shoulders back and down, his arms hanging loose by his sides. Like a neon sign hung over his head, saying: *innocent and nonthreatening!*

"Officer." Otis nodded, his nostrils flaring as he recognized a fellow shifter. Not a wolf, though; a big cat of some kind, judging by the scent.

His human face was familiar too—brown eyes and wild tawny hair. Handsome. Otis thought he'd maybe seen the cop before, laughing with Bree and her friends in the bar. Jealousy surged hot through his veins, but he tamped it down with the ease of practice.

Otis got jealous a lot around Bree. He prided himself on the fact no one noticed.

"Thank you for coming." The cop nodded to the Silver Bullet owner, the old windbag still ranting without pause, and walked away while the guy was mid-sentence. It made Otis like him just a tiny bit more. Just an inch. "We've received an accusation against your pack. That you're responsible for this damage. While many creatures could be responsible"—he threw a pointed look at the old biker—"we have to follow up on every lead."

"Understood." Otis didn't like it, but he could respect it. Sort of. "Is this an official interview? Do I need a lawyer?"

He didn't have one, but it sure sounded good. And the cop looked alarmed, shaking his head.

"No. These are informal questions."

Otis felt rather than heard Bree walk up behind him. She stopped at his elbow, a few inches from his side. Did she notice the way she always wound up standing beside him? The way she drifted toward him, pulled by an invisible current? Even when they were in a group, out with her friends and the vampire from his radio station, Bree always inched subconsciously nearer.

He wouldn't ask. If he knew anything about Bree, it was that once she noticed, she'd fight the urge to be close to him tooth and nail.

"The werewolves are tall." Bree spoke casually, but Otis could feel the tension radiating off her. It pissed her off that he was here, and not just because he annoyed her no end. She was *defensive* of him. Interesting. "All of them. They're all over six feet."

"So?" the bar owner barked, but the cop nodded, glancing at the door. Whatever she was saying, he was picking up. He gestured for Otis to stand next to the door, and Otis went gamely. He had nothing to hide.

"See?" Bree said, triumphant, and the cop nodded again. "Danny, come on. It wasn't him."

Danny. They were friendly, then. On a first name basis. Otis ground his teeth and forced the smile to stay on his face.

He would not be a territorial asshole. He would not be one of *those* men. Even if this shifter had broad shoulders and a chiselled face, and Bree called him *Danny*.

"Anyone want to clue me in?" Otis asked, voice pleasant. Bree huffed, but grabbed his forearm in her hands. His skin tingled under her warm, dry palms as she moved his hand in a slashing motion beside the door. He had to stoop to reach the bottom of the claw marks, his face bending closer to hers. She smelled like leather and dark cherries.

"See?" Bree sounded breathless. Either she was just as affected by him, or his arm was heavy. "You're too tall. Even shifted, this wouldn't be comfortable."

Otis took pity on her, straightening up and pulling his arm free. It was true—even on all fours as a wolf, he'd tower over these marks.

"He's the biggest one." The bar owner talked like Otis wasn't even here. The grizzly old bastard wouldn't even look at him. "The smaller ones could have done it."

Danny sighed, like he thought that was bullshit, but nodded again. Bree had proved nothing. Nothing, except that she secretly cared.

Otis leaned down to whisper in her ear as the other two men headed inside to inspect the damage.

"Don't worry, Mendez." Damn it, no matter how Otis tried, he couldn't help but needle her. "Your secret is safe with me."

"What secret?" She jerked her head away, crossing her arms over her chest. A frown creased her forehead, and she glowered at the claw marks gouged through the wood.

"Oh, you know. The worst kept secret in all of Boiling River. That no matter how much you claim to hate me, you find me irresistible."

Bree scoffed and stomped inside, her thick leather boots crunching broken glass to powder. Otis grinned and followed after.

She could deny it as much as she liked, but he knew the truth. He felt it with every thump of his heart in his chest.

His fated mate couldn't ignore the pull for much longer.

Irresistible.

13

Chapter 3

"*G*ods, I hate his guts. Otis *Pascale*. What kind of name is that?"

Bree stabbed at the crushed ice in the bottom of her glass, her straw chewed and buckling. Empty glasses littered the marble-top breakfast bar, along with bottle caps and cartons of half-eaten Chinese takeout. Across the kitchen, leaning gracefully against the fridge, Zacharias winced as his eyes skated over the wreckage.

Too bad. The vamp shouldn't have volunteered his lair for girls' night. Bree waited until he caught her eye, then sucked long and loud at the dregs in her cocktail.

"Bree." Claire huffed a laugh, sliding off her stool and crossing to Zacharias. She wound her arms around his waist, rested her head on his shoulder, and shot him the most disgustingly adoring look Bree had ever seen. "Don't torment him."

"I'm not tormented." The vampire sounded vaguely offended, but a faint smile played over his smile as he tugged at Claire's red hair. "She can be as disgusting as she likes. It's girls' night."

"Exactly." Bree slid off her stool, her heeled boots thudding against the tiles. "See? He's the gatecrasher, Claire Bear." Her footsteps rang out as she crossed to the sound system, twiddling the dials and cranking up the volume. Music hummed through the speakers, wild and reckless, and Bree moved her hips to the beat.

Gods, she needed this tonight. After losing that shift, spending a humiliating hour on the phone to her bank, dealing with that *man*—

"It's his apartment."

"What?" Bree blinked over her shoulder. "Who?"

Claire snorted, shaking her head, and Zacharias leaned down to whisper in her ear. Bree watched as his lips grazed her skin; saw the way her friend sucked in a breath as her pupils dilated.

Gross. This was why they didn't bring dates to girls' night. Yes, okay, it was the vamp's apartment, but didn't he have anywhere else to go?

Like the radio station, for example. With that ass of a werewolf.

"Are you okay?"

Bree barely heard Olivia's whisper over the pounding music. It took a second for the question to filter through her jagged thoughts, then she glanced over to the girl huddled on her stool.

Olivia. The quiet one. The sweet one, out of the three of them. And for the last six months, the girl with dark shadows under her eyes. No matter how they asked her, she wouldn't—or couldn't—tell them what was going on. Only that she wasn't sleeping well.

Even now, bundled up in a cream sweater and a soft blue

scarf, Olivia was trembling. Her cheeks were hollow and her lips dry.

Bree sucked her teeth, flapping a hand.

"Of course I'm okay. I always am." She grabbed Olivia's elbow and tugged her down off the stool. She didn't miss the way Olivia's eyes darted to the speakers, her cheeks paling. She'd planned on making Olivia dance, but something about that terrified look set Bree on edge. She walked over to the speaker and slapped the sound off completely.

"Let's play poker," she announced instead. They all needed a distraction.

There was a vicious satisfaction in beating a vampire at cards. Zacharias studied his hand, his features carefully blank, and made every play with the impression of full control. Compared to Olivia—distracted—and Claire—impulsive—he was a master player.

"Too bad you never learned to play in your couple of centuries." Bree smirked as she lay down her cards, her eyes fixed on Zacharias as he stared at her hand. His gaze flicked up, his eyes narrowing. Yeah, this was a great idea.

"You cheated."

Bree tutted. "Don't be a sore loser." A muscle ticked in the vampire's jaw, and Bree grinned.

This wasn't the man Bree really wanted to tear apart. The one she carried around all this pent up frustration for. But Zacharias was nearby, convenient, and hilarious when he got in a mood. He glanced at Claire, as if to see whether she'd jump to his defense again.

Claire shrugged. "She beat you. Pay up, vamp."

Zacharias sighed and stood to fix them more drinks—a process Bree watched with leisurely enjoyment. She was in her mid-twenties, way past when it was exciting to work in a bar, and she still poured drinks for a living. One of the best parts of girls' night was someone else making the drinks for a change.

Bree chewed on her thumbnail, her gaze skating over the vampire's shiny kitchen appliances. His fully stocked cupboards; his top of the range sound system. If she turned her head, she'd see his freaking pool. Like most immortals, Zacharias had untold riches.

He'd probably never spent an hour on the phone with his bank, getting lectured by some guy in a suit.

And even beside his wealth, Zacharias had a job. A skilled job. A *career*. Claire was an artist; Olivia was a librarian. Even Danny was a fully trained cop.

Only Bree had failed to grow up. She accepted the fresh drink with subdued thanks, swirling the straw in the crushed ice. The scent of fresh mint and lime drifted over her cheeks, and she sucked in a breath.

What the hell was she doing with her life? Why couldn't she make herself leave Boiling River? She'd tried so many times, and every time, the town dragged her back. Away from all the jobs she could have tried for; all the lives she could have built.

Bree couldn't explain it. There was nothing here for her besides her friends, and they'd be close no matter where she lived. Yet every time she spent too long away from the desert valley, an ache started in her chest.

Something tickled at her brain—a whispered answer—but she pushed it away. She wasn't ready for it yet. Bree pushed back her shoulders, chugged a mouthful of cocktail, and slapped the counter.

"Alright. Who's up for round two?"

* * *

"You don't have to do that." Zacharias looked faintly amused, plucking a dirty glass out of her hand. Bree stood in his kitchen, the dishwasher propped open, filling the trays with dirty glasses.

"I can't help it." She swiped another glass off the counter, this one stained with the telltale red of a Bloody Mary. A droplet of blood gathered on the rim as she upended it in the dishwasher. "I see a dirty glass, I clean it. It's compulsive at this point."

Zacharias huffed, the soft exhalation of his laugh taking Bree by surprise. They weren't enemies, exactly. They had one crucial thing in common: loving Claire. But Bree's spiky personality put the vampire on guard, and she hadn't particularly tried to set him at ease again.

"I worked the bar once. In New York."

Bree whistled. "A fancy place?"

"Nope. It was back in the twenties. A speakeasy."

Bree blinked. She knew, of course, that Zacharias was a vampire and over two centuries old. But somehow knowing that fact and comprehending the reality were two separate things.

Of course he was alive in the twenties. Of course he dressed differently; spoke differently; drove those clunky old cars.

"Why work in a bar?" The question needled at her sometimes. He had all this money; why work at all? "I thought the whole point of being a vamp is being disgustingly wealthy."

"It is," Zacharias agreed, voice light. They spoke quietly—out in the living space, Claire and Olivia slumped together on the sofa, dozing in front of the silent credits of a movie. "But eternity is a long time to fill. I find it helpful to have some

18

purpose."

"I wouldn't work in a bar." Zacharias slid her a funny look, but Bree shrugged. "If I had eternity, I wouldn't spend it pouring other people's drinks."

"What would you do, then?" He bent over, pulling the front of the dishwasher closed. Around them, the countertops were empty except for spills. Bree grabbed a cloth and spray bottle and started wiping.

What would she do? If she was an immortal creature, desperately seeking purpose? The same thoughts scrolled across her mind that she'd had a thousand times before—traveling, learning guitar, working in an animal shelter. Hell, if she was really brave, maybe even starting her own business. There were a hundred and one things Bree wanted to do with her life, and here she was not doing any of them.

Her chest throbbed.

"I don't know." She forced a smirk for Zacharias. "Guess that's why I work at Silver Bullet."

He hummed, drumming his fingers on the counter.

"I could ask Otis if you like. About a job in Supernatural Airwaves…?"

"No." Olivia shifted on the sofa. Bree lowered her voice and schooled her tone. "No. Thanks. I'm not supernatural, remember?"

"That doesn't matter—"

She cut across him. "And I like where I am."

It was such a blatant lie, such a shameless brush off, that Zacharias didn't bother to argue. He nodded, grabbed a cloth, and wiped down the other counter, his back to her. Bree took longer than needed, scrubbing hard at the surface long after the spills were gone. His offer bounced around her head, and her heart jangled in her chest, the metallic taste of panic still strong in her mouth.

No. She couldn't ask Otis Pascale for a job. She didn't want to work in radio, anyway. And she hadn't told Zacharias the most important detail: it was Otis she kept trying to get away from.

Chapter 4

O tis scratched his beard and frowned at the pack of werewolves in his living room. They were crammed in shoulder to shoulder, the two biggest on his sofa and the rest perched on chairs, tables, and his rug. Some of them had come straight from the Boiling River boxing gym, their skin slick with sweat under their vest tops and their scent muggy. Otis opened a window.

His cabin was small, modeled off the mountain retreat he used to hike to in the winters with his father, and it was not built with twelve burly werewolves in mind. That was his mistake. He'd known he was an alpha long before he built his home here. But a stubborn, sentimental part of him insisted on recreating his dad's cabin, seating arrangements be damned.

"You've all heard about Silver Bullet." It wasn't a question. Werewolf packs were worse than grandmas' knitting circles for gossip. As soon as Otis sent that message about alibis, there were sure to be keen eyes and strained ears in the area.

A series of nods spread through the room like ripples. Good.

He wouldn't have to rehash the mess of this morning.

"You know the old man thinks we did it."

One of the younger wolves snarled, jerking his chin up. He was folded on the rug, all knees and elbows, his hair damp with sweat.

"What's the old bastard's problem?"

The newest pups were often the most defensive. They'd just had the life they'd always known torn away from them, their bodies forced to shift in new and terrifying ways, and they took to the pack with religious fervor.

It was also usually the young ones causing problems, getting out of control.

Otis raised a palm. "His business was attacked. There were claw marks on his door. Of course he's suspicious." A low grumble went around the room, and Otis shrugged, his mouth tugging up. "That, and he's a crusty old bigot."

The pup who spoke—Jason—grinned, elbowing the guy sitting next to him. His neighbor was a coyote shifter, and the only non-wolf in the pack. He'd turned up on Otis' doorstep one night, his frayed beanie clutched in his hands.

"Please," was all he'd said, his throat working as he tried to swallow. "I can't do this alone."

He didn't have to ask twice. None of them did. Otis was a sucker for a lost pup. And though there'd been some tension in the pack, some aggravated whispers, Otis stared at the gossipers until they shut the hell up.

He was the alpha. His pack; his rules. Otis would never force anyone to stay against their will, but for those who stuck around, his word was law.

Lucky for them, he wasn't the despotic type. The most he asked of them was a weekly barbecue and good behavior.

"I need your alibis for last night. And we're on pack lock-down for the next week. If there's another attack, I want everyone accounted for. Not just by other pack members, either—stay public and visible." He nodded at the coyote shifter. "Micah will coordinate. Check in with him as you go."

As alpha, it was his right to pick his second in command. Usually, that meant a big, burly wolf who could hold his back in battle. But Otis was a peaceful guy, and the next biggest wolf was a local guy named Pedro. In his fifties, Pedro suffered from a laundry list of ailments, including a fear of blood, a gangrenous leg, and a bee allergy.

Pedro was relieved not to be chosen. He shifted on the sofa, the cushions flattening under his bulk.

"You want us to look around? See who mighta done it?"

Otis didn't think Pedro knew the day of the week.

"Good idea," was all he said, nodding at the older wolf. "I'll look into it myself."

The last thing they needed was a bunch of overeager wolves sniffing around the crime scene. Especially not Jason and the other pups with their bitter streak. He couldn't blame them—when they shifted, everyone looked at them differently, even if they grew up here. No wonder they got wound up and knocked over the local trash cans. No wonder they spray painted the back of the library that time.

Otis understood it all, but that didn't mean he could go soft. He made them scrub that spray paint off by hand and write an apology letter to the librarian.

Micah watched him, green eyes sharp. Otis tipped his head at him, just a fraction.

They'd deal with it. The two of them. And if the other wolves didn't like a coyote as a second in command, they could find another pack.

* * *

"This doesn't feel like a random attack." Micah waited until the pack were tearing into a massive order of meat feast pizzas, the cardboard boxes piled on every surface. He found Otis in the galley kitchen, twisting the cap off a beer. Otis nodded, taking a swig.

According to Officer *Danny*, nothing valuable was stolen. There was damage and destruction, but no theft. And those claw marks gouged into the front door, in full view of the street...

It was a message. For the bar owner; for the cops. For someone.

Otis hated seeing those marks so near Bree Mendez. The violence scored into the wood.. For a sickening moment, he wondered whether the message was for Bree... but it made no sense. She hadn't been rattled at all, only more pissed off than usual.

"There'll be another." He muttered so the other wolves wouldn't hear, but they were too busy yelling and eating with their mouths open. "That's why we're locking down. I want us kept out of it."

Micah nodded, his canny eyes flicking to the refrigerator. Otis sighed, pulling the fridge door open and pulling out another beer.

The coyote was twenty-two. It wasn't illegal. But he didn't want any of the pups crying favoritism.

"Drink that in here."

"Sure, boss."

Chapter 4

"And Micah?"

"Yeah?"

Otis scratched his chin, staring through the kitchen window to the pack. Wolves came and went from Boiling River, some moving here when they shifted, while others grew up here then left to see the world. Otis never tried to stop either process—he figured it was healthy to get fresh blood—and the pack always settled into its hierarchy after a few scuffles.

"Make sure you eat." He slid Micah a look. The coyote shifter fiddled with the label on his bottle. His reddish brown hair curled around his ears. He was leaner than the wolves, muscled but slender, and his green eyes were sharp and knowing. "Don't let them jump the line. You're second in command."

Otis didn't give a shit when he ate, even though he was supposed to go first, but no one questioned that he was the alpha. It was different for Micah. He had to hold his own.

Micah sighed. "I'm not even hungry."

"Take the dough balls, then." The garlic dip was prized. It was as good a message to send as any.

Micah sighed again, like the weight of the world lay on his shoulders, then strode out of the kitchen and into the fray. He plucked the box of dough balls out of Jason's hands and snarled when the wolf tried to take them back.

Micah settled on a stool on the edges of the pack, not in the thick of it but not pushed away either. He'd taken his beer too, but maybe that was a good thing. Micah swigged from the bottle, eyeing the wolves pointedly.

Yeah. Otis grinned from the kitchen, scratching his thumbnail over his own bottle. Micah would be fine.

* * *

25

It took four hours to get the pack out of his cabin. They took forever to eat, then raided his cupboards for more snacks, then insisted on watching an old monster B-movie. By the time the last of them ducked through the front door, Otis was ready to chase them out with a broom.

He shook his head, propping the door open to let desert breeze in. It was cold in the valley at night, the temperatures plummeting, and goosebumps prickled over his skin as he looked out at the crescent moon. It shone over the mountain tops, the sky dusted with stars, and the desert quiet but for the cry of hunting owls.

Otis wandered onto his porch, resting his forearms on the wooden railing. He'd done this on purpose—built his cabin ass-backwards. If he walked down the wooden steps and circled round the building, he'd find the Boiling River town sprawled behind him. But this way, he could come out onto his porch and see only wilderness.

It wasn't the damp, pine-fresh forests he'd hiked through with his dad, but it was close enough. Only the lights of the Starlight Springs wellness retreat shone partway up the valley, clustered on a ledge. He'd tried to climb that rock face once, plotting routes up the cliff, but the smooth rock had beaten him back.

He didn't mind. Otis was patient.

Crickets chirped in the sparse grasses, and a bigger animal huffed from the shadows. Probably one of his wolves, or another shifter. No wild animal would be foolish enough to encroach on his territory. The bears and mountain lions gave him a wide berth.

The chorus of insects and the blanket of stars—they hypnotized him somehow. Otis stood out on that porch, lost in snow-packed memories of his father, feeling the remembered crunch of snow under his boots. The stars spun lazily across the sky overhead, their lights pulsing through the darkness, and Otis leaned against the railing, lost in thought.

He only came back to himself when the hairs stood up on his neck. He was being watched.

This was different from the cautious perusal of another shifter. From the wide-eyed stare of the owls which nested in the giant cactus opposite. This was a sickly, vicious feeling—one that made his heart race and his teeth lengthen. Someone was watching him, their eyes filled with hate.

Otis didn't move an inch. He kept his eyes trained on the stars, his posture relaxed and fluid. He inhaled deeply through his nose, trying to catch a scent, but whoever it was stood downwind.

The feeling lasted for almost half an hour. Then, as quickly as it came, it was gone. Otis straightened up, clapping a hand on the railing, adrenaline still surging through his veins.

He'd told the pack to stay together to keep them out of trouble. But perhaps it was good to keep them on guard, too.

Someone was watching the wolves of Boiling River. Someone who'd gouged the front door of the Silver Bullet with enough force and hatred to buckle the wood.

Otis leaped down the steps to stroll the perimeter, his mind racing.

His pack was under threat.

Chapter 5

*B*ree crouched and lined up her shoulder with the toppled pool table, pressing her hands against the felt and gritting her teeth. With a grunt, she shoved her full weight into the table, the soles of her boots squeaking against the floor as the wood creaked and shifted.

It lifted an inch off the floor. Two inches. Bree bit her lip and pushed harder.

Then the table crashed back to the ground and slid along the bar floor.

"Shit." Bree shoved her hair out of her face, her chest heaving. Her skin was damp with sweat, her black t-shirt stuck to her back, and though she'd been sweeping up glass and righting furniture for hours, the Silver Bullet looked as wrecked as when she started this morning.

Charlton was nowhere to be seen—probably out bugging the Boiling River cops about the werewolves—and Bree had been left to deal with the fallout alone.

"Shit," Bree said again with feeling. This was a disaster.

"Need a hand?"

They were the right words, but said in the voice of the man Bree least wanted to see. She glanced at the familiar shape filling the buckled doorway.

Otis. His amber eyes creased in amusement, his wide mouth curling into a grin. With his short dark hair and the firm jawline under his beard, the man would look at home on the red carpet.

Instead he was here, pissing her off. Bree shook her head, not bothering to answer him. She turned back to the pool table, glaring at the scuff marks on the polished wood edge.

Charlton would ream her out about that. Gripe that she should have been more careful, when all the while he wasn't even here. Bree sighed, scrubbing her hands down her face, when a noise made her peek through her fingers.

Otis lifted the table easily, like it weighed no more than the bar stools, and set it the right way up. He dusted his hands off and turned to her, eyebrow raised.

"Thank you," Bree grumbled reluctantly.

She didn't want to be like this with him. She knew she was too harsh, that she ignored every white flag he offered her. Though Otis Pascale was a shameless tease, he was also unfailingly generous and kind.

Bree couldn't explain it. Something about him set her on edge. One look from those amber eyes, and she wanted to sprint straight into the desert screaming.

"Any time." Otis reached out and tugged her hair. *Right.* That was why she hated him. She batted him off, ignoring the warmth on her skin where their hands met.

"What are you doing here, Pascale? Sightseeing?"

"Something like that." Otis looked around the bar, his nostrils flaring as he inhaled deeply.

Sniffing for scents. Supernaturals were so weird. Bree rolled her eyes and picked up her broom.

"You didn't get a good enough look yesterday?" She threw the question over her shoulder, watching as Otis paced slowly through the bar, his broad shoulders tense and his fists clenched at his sides.

"No." Otis muttered at the floorboards, his deep voice carrying through the empty bar. "Not with Officer Danny stinking up the joint."

"Danny doesn't smell." Bree should know. She sat next to him at movie night last week. For some reason, that declaration made Otis' spine stiffen.

"He does to me," he said, voice clipped. Bree didn't think she'd ever heard him annoyed before. For some backwards reason, it cheered her up, and she danced over to him with a grin. Her broom dragged through the dust and shattered glass and wood splinters as she went, drawing a wobbly trail.

"You know what I think?" She nudged Otis' shoulder where he stood frowning at the dark wood bar. The surface was scratched and faded, stained by ancient spills, but Bree kept it damn clean, scrubbing until her elbow twinged every shift.

"What?" Otis barely looked at her, his voice distracted. His eyes were fixed on the cash register, his forehead creased. Bree leaned closer.

"I think you like Danny."

Otis hummed, then jerked his head to her, eyes wide.

"I do not," he spluttered, way too shaken. Bree rocked back on her heels, mouth sour. Her grip tightened on the broom.

"Why so horrified, Pascale? Is it because Danny's a man?"

"No." Now it was Otis' turn to look offended. "I'm not an

asshole. I have no problem with that."

"Then why?"

Otis rolled his eyes. For the first time in their acquaintance, he looked truly tired of her.

Panic squirmed through Bree's gut.

"I'm spoken for," was all he said, the words coming out clipped. He turned back to the cash register, the conversation over.

Spoken for. His words echoed through her head, and Bree looked down at the broom handle clutched in her hands. She swallowed, her mouth dry, and walked away to sweep under a table.

Spoken for.

What had she expected? Why was she so worked up? She didn't even like Otis Pascale. But reasonably, rationally, she could see that of course someone else would. He was handsome, funny, and friendly. He had a good job and was the alpha of a pack.

Otis had his life sorted out. He was everything she was not.

"I'm locking up in ten," she told him, her voice hoarse as her broom swept over the debris.

Otis grunted, the floorboards creaking under his boots as he rounded the bar. He poked through the shelves, opened the dishwasher, even flipped open the folder of Health and Safety forms.

Bree shrugged and kept sweeping, acting calmer than she felt.

This was why she didn't spend time with him. Otis knocked the ground out from under her.

* * *

The werewolves of Boiling River were not known for their good manners. Bree got the impression from the limited time she'd spent with the pack that Otis tried his best, drilling them to keep their instincts at bay. But it was like a single dad found himself raising twelve rowdy foster kids all alone, and even the best alpha would have his work cut out.

Trash cans were still knocked over. The library was spray painted. Vegetable patches were trampled.

And every time, Otis was livid, dragging the responsible wolf back to the scene by the ear.

She figured he'd boss her about more. Insist on staying and looking longer—maybe force her to stay late or just refuse to leave. But the moment Bree said she was heading home, Otis shoved his hands in his pockets and walked straight out to the street.

Weird. Bree shook her head, checking the register and the stockroom were locked out of habit before grabbing her leather jacket off the back of a chair. The evening air was cool on her cheeks when she stepped back into the street, shoving the splintered door shut behind her.

"You're still here." She slid the key in the lock, letting her hair fall forward and block her face. She'd fully expected Otis to disappear into the night, either on four legs or two.

"Yup. Figured I'd walk you home."

Bree snorted. "I know the way, thanks."

"Oh, yeah? Did you know there's a criminal on the loose?"

Bree shot him a look, but Otis was smiling. Teasing her again.

Bree gestured to the claw marks. "How do I know I'm not safer alone?" For a split second, Otis actually looked hurt. The expression flitted behind his eyes, almost too fast to see, and Bree wished she could stuff those words back in her mouth.

32

Then Otis beamed, throwing his arms wide. "I thought you liked to gamble, Mendez?"

He had a point. She huffed a laugh, falling into step beside him. He was taller than her, but he adjusted his stride, keeping pace with her without being asked. And as they walked, Bree realized they were breathing in sync, their chests rising and falling as one. She held her breath for half a step, deliberately breaking the rhythm, and Otis shot her a look.

"Have you forgotten how to walk? That's embarrassing."

"I have, actually. Bet you feel like a dick now."

They grinned at each other, falling into easy silence as they wound through the Boiling River streets. Most days, Bree rode her bike into work, but there was no way she'd leave her baby at the scene of a crime. No—her bike was tucked safely away at home, away from the prying eyes of vandals.

Plus, this was nice. Walking home in the evening with a werewolf at her side. The town was shutting up for the day, putting away its thin veneer of respectability. Across the street, the green grocer pulled the shutters down over his shop, and the Fae hairdresser locked up her shiny glass door.

Bodies spilled into the night. Tourists; locals; strangers. Boiling River was coming out to play.

"Let me guess," Otis said. "You're a night owl."

Bree glanced up at him, eyebrows raised.

"I work in a bar. That's not rocket science."

"That's not what I mean and you know it."

The thing was, Bree did know it. She'd always been happier in the shadows, in the wild hours between dusk and dawn. When she'd hit puberty and failed to change into a supernatural creature, she'd secretly wanted to demand a recount.

These creatures with their fangs and their claws and their

primal instincts—they were her people. No wonder she felt so out of place, like such a failure among the other humans.

"You're right," she said quietly. She didn't know why; she usually argued with Otis for the sake of it. But things felt different tonight, as the stars winked overhead, and creatures rustled and hissed in the dark alleys.

It felt good to be understood.

"I want to guess something." Otis hummed, encouraging her. She needed to even this playing field. One of the reasons the werewolf pissed her off so much was that she always felt like he knew something she didn't.

Something about her. Bree hated being kept in the dark.

"You're…" Bree fumbled for something to say. Something to prove she paid attention, too. She snapped her fingers. "You have daddy issues."

His laugh was strangled. "Excuse me? Is this about Danny again?"

"No." She kicked at a bone on the sidewalk. "But anyone who collects that many strays has issues."

Otis was quiet for a moment. More serious than she'd ever seen him.

Then he said, "My father died when I was fourteen. Once he was gone, I had no one. I miss him every day."

Bree should have known to guess something else. It did not feel good to be right. She bit her lip and looked up at the stars, glittering in the darkness, watching their every move.

"I'm sorry."

"It's okay."

They walked ten more steps together. Twenty.

Bree said, "My family are gone too. They're not dead or anything, but they left me behind." She stared down at her boots. There was a scuff mark on one toe.

"Why didn't you go with them?" Of course Otis knew the story. Knew how Bree's family packed up and moved west when she was eighteen, and she refused to go too.

She couldn't explain it then and she couldn't now. She didn't even like Boiling River all that much. All she knew was that it was important she stay here. She felt it to the marrow of her bones.

Bree shrugged. She could hardly tell him that; Otis would check her into the nearest padded cell.

"Unfinished business here, I guess."

One day, she'd be done with it, she vowed. She would leave.

They fell silent again, rounding the corner to her street, both lost in their thoughts as they approached her apartment. Otis sensed something first, his head jerking up and his nose sniffing the air.

"Oh, shit," he said, his voice thick as his teeth lengthened in his mouth. Bree followed the line of his vision, her mouth dropping open as she saw her apartment.

Her windows were busted. Her bike was toppled over into the street.

And her home was on fire.

Chapter 6

"**S**hit. Oh my gods. *Shit.*" Bree lunged forward, ready to... what? Scale the walls? Put the fire out by sheer force of will? Otis wouldn't put it past her. Hell, if the need to protect her didn't burn constantly through his veins, he'd stand back and enjoy the show.

"Stay here."

He held out an arm, barring Bree from walking further down the sidewalk. She scoffed, trying to get past him, her eyes glued on the flickering light in her bedroom window, but he gripped her shoulders, giving her a little shake until she met his eye.

"Let me take a look first. Alright?" She opened her mouth to argue, but Otis held up a hand. "Wolves are much harder to kill. You know that, Mendez."

Indecision warred in her brown eyes, but she stayed put, forehead creased.

Good. The gods knew Otis loved this woman, but she was not known for keeping a cool head. He tugged his gray long-sleeved t-shirt over his head, pushing it into her hands. The night air nipped at his bare chest, his nipples pebbling in the cold, and Otis avoided Bree's gaze as he toed off his work boots and undid his belt buckle.

"Do you mind?" he said at last when she kept staring, her eyes wide like saucers. Bree jerked, spinning around, her cheeks flaming, and Otis stifled a grin.

She didn't find him *that* repulsive.

"It gets expensive," he told her as he folded his jeans and passed them to her. She took them without looking, piling them with his shirt. "Tearing through clothes all the time. It's wasteful. And I'm shit at sewing."

"Uh-huh." Bree's shoulders were tense, bunched around her ears, but he didn't have time to tease her. Down the street, her apartment windows glowed orange, and black smoke billowed around the side of the building.

"Stay here," he repeated, screwing his eyes shut as his limbs lengthened and bent the wrong way; as fur burst from beneath his skin and his jaw cracked and grew.

The shift had been painful at first. A horrible, invasive shock. His body was not his own anymore, and he couldn't get his limbs to work properly. Couldn't make sense of his new, heightened senses. Truthfully, Otis still hated the shift itself—it gave him motion sickness. But when he opened his eyes again, his vision sharper and the trails of scents painted through the air, he shook himself and growled in satisfaction.

There was no safer place for Bree than with his werewolf form.

He glanced back at her, tongue lolling, before he took off at a trot down the sidewalk. A few residents glanced at him through their living windows then turned back to their TV screens. A werewolf was nothing to gape at in Boiling River;

there were far weirder things to spy out in the street.

As he drew closer to Bree's apartment, the sidewalk stayed cool beneath his paws. The fire was new, then, recently set, and he raised his nose to sniff at the air. The sidewalk was a tangle of scents, the trails of dozens of locals knotting together in an impossible mess. Otis huffed, ducking his head and trotting faster.

He'd find out more inside.

Bree lived in an old apartment building, and not the fancy kind. The stone was crumbling, the wooden door frames and window panes cracked and splintered, and most of the apartment windows were covered with hung sheets or propped up cardboard. Bree's apartment was one of the few with blinds—midnight blue blinds painted with moons and stars, courtesy of her artist buddy.

Otis probably shouldn't know that. He couldn't bring himself to feel ashamed.

Shattered glass crackled under his paws, prodding at his leathery pads but failing to break through the thick skin. The front door of the apartment building hung crooked on its hinges, the same claw marks gouged into the wood as at the bar. Inside, smoke clouded against the ceiling of the narrow hallway, and Otis crouched low, straining to listen.

TVs blared in the building. Radios hummed. Bree's neighbors hadn't noticed the smoke yet, the silent, toxic fog filling their hallways. Soon, their thin walls would heat, the paint starting to sweat, and they'd be trapped in their homes. Sitting ducks waiting to be cooked.

Three floors up, a baby wailed.

Otis turned to face the street, raised his head, and howled.

Chapter 6

* * *

The other wolves answered his call instantly, streaking through the darkening streets. Micah arrived first, the top of his furry head barely reaching Otis' belly. He breathed hard, his sides ballooning with each lungful, but he fell straight into rhythm, following Otis' lead instinctively. They barged apartments doors open, yipping and barking for the neighbors to get out, and though more than one resident ran at them with a frying pan, they soon noticed the smoke and got the message.

One by one, the other wolves joined, until the building's residents gathered on the sidewalk with Bree—a colorful huddle of work uniforms, house coats and hairnets. Bree watched everything, her face pale and Otis' clothes clutched to her chest. When he came out with the baby and its mother, escorting them right to the sidewalk, Bree swallowed with an audible gulp.

Good. Otis preened, his fur puffing up. About time she saw him as more than just a pain in her ass.

By the time the town fire truck pulled up, the building was nearly empty. Otis called back his pack with a yip, gathering together on the sidewalk and watching through amber eyes as the firefighters ran into the building. They were brave men and women—humans and supernaturals alike—and for the first time since arriving, Otis sat back on his haunches and let himself think. This was under control.

He'd been so distracted evacuating the building, he'd forgotten to check Bree's apartment. To scent the air and find out who set that fire.

Because it was deliberate. That much was clear, from the claw marks gouged in the front door. And it was definitely her apartment where the fire had been set—he recognized the starry sky blinds, half closed on the orange glow.

Who the hell wanted to hurt his bartender? Bree had plenty of flaws—he wasn't blind—but none that would inspire this kind of hate. She had no secret riches, no underground connections... she was just Bree.

His Bree.

Otis growled, rising to his paws and stalking to where she huddled with her neighbors. She watched him approach, mouth slightly open, and when he shifted back to his human form, she held out his clothes without a word. Otis stepped into his jeans quickly, fastening his belt as he shoved his feet into his boots, one eye on her and one on the apartment. Over Bree's shoulder, a cop car pulled up and Officer Danny lunged into the street.

"What happened?" The leopard shifter's brown eyes were hard as he approached them. Accusatory. A growl rumbled through Otis' chest.

"A bank heist," Bree snapped, her gaze focused again. "What the hell do you think happened, Danny?"

Otis grinned, the points of his fangs digging into his lip as he shrugged his shirt over his head. He loved when Bree was vicious, and he loved it even more when it was aimed at this asshole.

"There." He pointed at Bree's window. "Someone set the fire in her apartment. Look." He dragged his hand to point at the front door. "It's a message."

Danny nodded, his jaw tight. He pulled his radio from his belt, muttering codes and instructions in clipped tones. When he was done, he shoved the radio back on his belt and turned to Bree.

"Are you okay?"

Otis bristled. That was his line.

"I'm fine. I didn't even go inside."

"They must have known you weren't there," Danny mused, staring up at the glowing orange window. As one, the gathered crowd flinched as the pane blew out, smoke billowing up to the sky.

"Like I said." Otis stepped closer to Bree's side. "A message."

Danny grunted, his face troubled. When he turned to Bree, his expression was so filled with concern, Otis wanted to wring his neck.

It was ridiculous. An ugly instinct, and one that Otis tamped down. But he still ground his teeth.

"Do you have somewhere you can go? Somewhere to stay the night?"

"Yes," Otis said before she could speak. Bree tossed him a glare which dripped with disdain.

"Did he ask you?"

Otis shrugged. "I'm just saying. You have plenty of options."

It was true. Bree had plenty of friends—she was the kind of carefree, generous person that attracted others like moths to a lamp. Claire would house her in a heartbeat, and so would the shy librarian, Olivia. Hell, even Angie or Zacharias would take her in without pause.

That wasn't what he'd meant, though. Not really. Otis wanted her at his cabin. Because he wanted her, yes, so badly his eyes practically crossed, but mostly because of the danger.

Someone wanted to hurt Bree. To hurt his mate. He needed to protect her.

Danny glanced between the two of them, his eyebrows quirked, then held up his palms like he didn't want to get into it.

"As long as you're set," he muttered to Bree, then strode off to find one of the firefighters.

She turned to him, arms crossed over her chest. Good thing the fire truck was near, because Bree looked ready to breathe flames.

"You don't speak for me." She jabbed him in the chest as she spoke, her nail digging into his muscle.

"Why?" Otis asked, irrationally annoyed. "Did you want to stay with Officer Danny?"

"It's none of your damn business who I stay with!"

"It is when there's a psycho after you!" Otis broke off, breathing hard, suddenly aware of the whispers around them. He leaned in, speaking quieter, forcing each word between clenched teeth. "I have to protect you, Bree. You know that."

It was the closest they'd ever come to acknowledging… this. The truth of what really lay between them. Not simple rivalry or antagonism, or at least, not just that.

She knew what she was to him. What they were to each other. She *knew* it.

And she could ignore it if she liked. It tore him up inside, but she had that damn right. Otis would respect her decision.

She didn't have to be with him. Didn't have to accept him as her mate. But by the gods, she would allow him to protect her.

This was the one and only instinct that Otis could not control.

Chapter 7

*B*ree clasped her hands together and held them under her chin.

"Please tell me this was an accident. Please tell me that Otis Pascale, the alpha of Boiling River, built his house back to front by mistake."

"If it makes you happy."

The werewolf beamed, grabbing her hand and tugging her round the side of the cabin. He didn't seem the slightest bit offended, his eyes still gleaming bright with the triumph of persuading her to stay with him.

It wasn't much of a fight, really. The destruction of her apartment rattled Bree more than she let on, and whatever else she felt about Otis, the man made her feel safe.

She trusted him to protect her. But she wasn't ready to admit why just yet.

It was… too much. Too big. The ramifications for her, for the rest of her life—they were huge. And her world had already tilted on its axis today, her shabby but cozy apartment going up in flames in front of her eyes.

Bree had lived there since she was seventeen. Eight years of her life were gathered in that apartment, woven into the clutter on her shelves and the photos pinned to her walls. Charlton had rented it to her the week her family took off for the west coast, leaving a heartbroken Bree in their wake.

Now it was gone. Maybe only for a few weeks; maybe forever. No one knew the extent of the damage just yet. But even if she could move back in tomorrow, the safety she'd once felt there was shattered.

Bree couldn't go back. It wasn't her home anymore.

She'd daydreamed so many times about being untethered—about cutting all her ties to Boiling River and setting herself loose in the world. And now someone was snipping those ties for her, one by one.

Her job. Her home.

What else was there to cut?

"Charlton owns that apartment," Bree said, as casually as she could, as they rounded the werewolf's cabin to the front steps. Otis glanced at her, eyes narrowed, the wooden porch creaking under his weight.

"You think this is about him?"

Bree shrugged. "I think he pisses off way more people than I do." Charlton was loud in his dislike for the town's supernatural community. At one point, he'd taken to hanging political posters in the Silver Bullet window, until too many customers complained.

Bree was relieved to take them down. She didn't like them either.

"An impressive feat." Otis winked as he dug his keys out of his pocket. He raised his nose and sniffed the air before they walked inside. No matter how many years Bree lived in Boiling River, no matter how many supernaturals she considered friends, it still took her off guard at times.

The man beside her was not fully human.

Something like envy swirled in Bree's gut as she followed him inside the cabin. It was small—way smaller than she'd expected for the alpha of a wolf pack. It reminded her of those basic wood cabins you saw on National Parks posters. There was no ostentation here, no declaration of status—just simple comfort, and the wide open air.

"Not what you had in mind?" Otis tilted his head, watching her reactions. She stepped past him, her footsteps muffled by a woven rug, one hand reaching out to touch a squat leather sofa. It was an open space: a wood burner surrounded by a cluster of sofas and armchairs, and a TV screen screwed on the wall. The wall to the galley kitchen was cut away, revealing basic appliances and a large fruit bowl on the counter.

There were magnets on the fridge. Paperback books crammed on the shelves lining the walls. This was a home.

Bree cleared her throat.

"I don't know." The words came out shakier than she'd intended. "I guess I figured there'd be more chew toys."

Otis snorted. "There's a dog bed in the bedroom. And a puppy pen out back."

"Seriously?"

Otis shrugged. "We are what we are."

One thing she secretly liked about Otis was that he was never apologetic for being a wolf. He was a werewolf, an alpha, the head of a radio station, and a shameless fan of dad jokes. What you saw with Otis was what you got.

Bree averted her eyes.

Otis spoke up, filling the silence for her.

"I'll get you some clothes to sleep in. There's a spare unopened toothbrush in the bathroom." Bree nodded along as he spoke, giving her a whistle-stop tour to his cabin. Urging her to help herself to whatever she needed.

Gods, she'd been an ass to this man.

"Otis." She caught his sleeve as he made to leave the room, crossing to the bedroom to grab himself a pillow. He insisted on being the one to sleep on the sofa, despite being twice the length of it.

He turned to her, eyes knowing, and waited for her to speak.

Bree licked her lips. "Thank you."

It was the most straightforward interaction they'd ever had. No needling each other, no winding each other up on purpose. Just one friend doing a favor for another.

Otis nodded and pulled his arm away.

"You're welcome."

For some reason, Bree's heart sank as she watched him leave the room. She didn't know what she'd expected, what she'd hoped for him to say—only that it wasn't that.

Bree wrapped her arms around her waist, dropped onto the sofa, and tried not to think about her situation. The sudden unemployment, the bank manager waiting to ream her out on the phone, her charred belongings… it could all wait.

Bree was good at avoiding things. She had a lot of practice.

* * *

How did you sleep when your life had literally gone up in flames? Bree tossed in the bed, moonlight shining through the window and bathing the sheets in a silver glow. She should probably shut the curtains, but it was hard to be cautious when there was a protective werewolf guarding her door.

His mattress was firm. The sheets were soft, brushed cotton, and a calming dove gray color. Bree rolled onto her front, burying her face in the pillow, and tried not to breathe him in.

His scent was everywhere. Even her measly human nose could smell him on every surface in this room. His bedroom was small but not cramped, filled only with a double bed, an oak closet, and a small writing desk. It had taken every inch of Bree's willpower not to pry through his things—to flick through the select few paperbacks stacked by his bed, or open the bedside drawer and peer inside.

Otis Pascale. She was in the alpha's bed. Bree groaned into the pillow, shaking her head.

Life was freaking weird.

She gave it two hours. Two hours of staring at the ceiling, of breathing his light, masculine smell into her nose. Then Bree huffed, threw the bed covers back, and stomped across the bedroom.

The door creaked on its hinges as she nudged it open. The lights were off, the only illumination coming from the glowing embers in the wood burner. Otis sat on the rug, his back leaned against the sofa, his eyes troubled as he stared into the fire.

Bree hovered. Had he heard her? Surely with his senses he knew she was here. She could fetch a glass of water from the kitchen and lock herself back in the bedroom, pretend she never saw the troubled crease to his brow...

"Come in, you creep." Otis slid her a wry smile. The firelight danced over his smooth brown face. "I know you haven't been sleeping."

"Now who's the creep?" Bree padded into the living room,

47

a blue knit throw draped around her shoulders. One of his t-shirts hung to her mid-thigh, the hem of his boxer shorts hidden beneath. Otis' eyes fixed on the sight of her in his clothes, his irises darkening.

Bree cleared her throat. "Down, boy."

Otis tossed his head back and laughed, shifting over on the rug and making space for her beside him. Bree lowered herself down, drawing up her knees and wrapping the ends of the throw around her legs.

"Want to talk about it?"

"Nope."

Otis nodded, not surprised at all. Bree chewed on her bottom lip. It couldn't be easy for him, always offering himself to her and getting knocked back. She used to wish he'd get the message and leave her alone.

Now the thought made her stomach clench.

"I couldn't sleep."

Otis flicked a piece of fluff off his knee. He still wore his jeans and sweater, his feet bare by the fire.

"Yeah, we covered that."

She nudged him with her shoulder.

"I'm trying, okay?"

"Okay." The smile he gave her was so warm, she heated from the inside out. "I'm glad you're trying."

"Me too." Bree rested her chin on her knees. She gusted out a breath. "I'm not good at this stuff, you know."

"I do know, yes." She darted a glance at him, but he didn't seem pissed. A bit sad, maybe, his eyes old as he stared into the fire.

"Maybe I just need time," Bree whispered. Her toes scrunched against the rug. Otis looked at her, his eyebrows raised, and something like hope dawning on his face. That much alone nearly sent her running screaming from his cabin, the pressure all too much.

"Sure." Otis nodded, then looked away quickly, like he could sense her getting spooked. "Maybe. I guess we'll see."

It would have to be enough. It was all she could offer him right now, and it was light years ahead of where they'd ever been before. She was here, after all, staying the night in his cabin when there were so many other places she could have gone.

She wore his t-shirt. She'd rolled in sheets laden with his scent. Even now, the outside of their legs were almost touching.

"You're a patient man," Bree mumbled, watching the embers pop and swirl.

"Not a man." He nudged her again. "A patient wolf."

That envy sliced through her again, but it was weaker this time. Muffled and distant.

Perhaps she wasn't supernatural. But he'd said himself: she was still a creature of the night.

Chapter 8

If there was a simple way to run a radio station, Otis hadn't found it yet. He sighed, leaning back in the chair in his office, scratching at his beard.

Four post-it notes with urgent memos decorated his computer monitor. Two of them, he couldn't remember who they were from or what they were about. One was illegible. His desk was clean, the surface wiped down, but the top drawer of the cabinet beside him was a secret shrine to mess.

There were looming bills stuffed in their envelopes. Dead batteries. Tangled paper clip chains. Six month old protein bars still in their wrappers.

Whenever Otis dared peek in his Drawer of Shame, he had a sinking feeling he knew why Bree didn't want him.

A boxy, cobwebbed speaker hung in the corner of the room, the faint strains of Supernatural Airwaves humming through the wire mesh. Kira, the station's weather girl, warned of hailstones in the valley and a stray tornado by the children's play park.

Otis sighed and grabbed his mug, tipping it back before realizing it was empty.

Coffee. That was the answer. Coffee would break this slump. Nine days out of ten, Otis was a creature of hope and laughter.

He was tired, that was all. In a slump. It would pass—it had to.

"Hey, boss man." A head poked into his office, halfway down the door frame. Angie, the station's cupid, grinned at him, her blunt chin-length hair swaying. "Want a fix?"

"Hell yes." Otis pushed away from his desk and stood. Angie's coffee's were legendary in Boiling River. Whenever someone asked about her secret ingredient, Angie winked and told them it was love.

Otis was no expert, but he figured it was more likely the triple pump of full-fat hazelnut.

"Stop." Angie held up a palm, eyes narrowing. "Stop right there."

Otis checked his fly.

"What? Why?"

"Something's wrong. There's something going on with you." The rest of Angie's body joined her head in his office. She propped her hands on her curvy hips, her pink scarf trailing to her knees. "Your heart is hurting."

Shit. This was the problem with having a cupid around. They could sniff out heartache like a bloodhound. Well, too bad for Angie, because Otis didn't feel like airing his dirty laundry for all to hear. They'd never look at him the same around the station if they knew he was a rejected mate. Hell, he might even lose his pack, and then what would happen to those pups?

Most days, he hid the ache well, buried it down deep where not even Angie noticed it. Apparently having Bree sleep over in his cabin dug up some stuff.

It was the toothbrush, he decided. Seeing her toothbrush in the cup next to his, and smelling her scent on his sheets. He'd almost been glad she refused to stay with him for the day, setting off toward the library to bother Olivia.

"I'm fine." Otis treated Angie to a megawatt smile. "Just some pack drama." By now, the whole town knew about the attacks, and the claw marks on the doors. An old lady crossed the street to avoid Otis this morning. "It'll work itself out."

Angie hummed, her face plainly saying she didn't buy it, but she'd let him lie if that made him feel better.

It did. It did make him feel better.

"Where's the vamp?" Otis asked as they stepped into the corridor, strolling toward the staff kitchen. Angie shot him a weird look.

"It's light outside."

"Right, right."

"Look." Angie grabbed his sleeve and dragged him to a halt. Over her shoulder, a ghost drifted through the wall and passed through the vending machine. "You can talk to me, okay? Not as a cupid. As a friend."

He punched her shoulder lightly. "I know that."

But how could he find words for something that had troubled him for so long? The constant ache for Bree was not news to Otis—it was his constant companion, a steady throb in his chest.

"We'll get a beer sometime," he offered. Angie sighed but nodded. They both knew Silver Bullet wouldn't open anytime soon.

It was okay. He'd drink Angie's coffee, then ride that sugar high all the way back to a good mood.

Chapter 8

***

"What happened?"

Otis raced across the ER, his boots thundering against the linoleum. The nurse at the desk saw him coming, holding up her palms to ward him off.

"He's in Room 5."

"What. Happened." Otis' rage and fear left a coppery taste in his mouth. The nurse prickled, her stooped shoulders pushing back and her wiry hair trembling as she raised her chin.

"I cannot give out confidential patient information, Mr. Pascale. He is in Room 5."

Otis growled and took off running again, raising his nose to sniff the air. The hospital was a tangle of scents, the trails of dozens of doctors and nurses criss-crossing through the halls while the smell of blood and antiseptic pulsed beneath. His heightened senses were useless. He almost barrelled straight past Room 5.

"In here," a voice called, and Otis snarled and changed direction, his tortured boots squeaking against the shiny floor.

Micah sat in a hospital bed, the flimsy gown stretched across his pale chest. Tubes ran from the back of his hand to a nearby machine, and rhythmic bleeps counted out his heartbeat.

"Shit." Otis lunged forward, only remembering to hold back his strength at the last second. He wrapped his arms around the younger man, ignoring Micah's protests and hugging him tighter.

"Gerroff," Micah mumbled into the front of Otis' sweater. He stepped back, scanning his beta for damage.

"Tell me." The words were clipped. A command. Micah began speaking at once.

53

"I was with Jason at the kiddie park. We were clearing everyone out because of the tornado, shuttling everyone indoors. I lost sight of Jason for a second, just while I ran round the back of the sports sheds, and someone hit me from behind."

Otis nodded and ran his fingers over the back of Micah's head, probing gently at the lump.

It was bad. Bloody and sore. If he were human, he'd be dead. Otis swallowed, his throat tight.

"Did you see who did it?"

Micah shook his head. "Neither did Jason. It all took maybe thirty seconds."

Otis sighed and stepped back, staring at the pale shifter in the hospital bed, before beginning to pace.

"There's one more thing."

Otis paused. He turned on his heel. Something about the way Micah spoke… this was going to be bad. His beta held something out—a metal chain which dangled from his grip. Otis reached for it, but Micah jerked it away.

Silver. Gods-damn it.

"They stuffed it in my mouth," Micah said, his tone calm, like it wouldn't have burned through his tongue if he'd been a true werewolf. "Must have thought I was one of the other pups."

"Shit." Otis screwed his eyes shut, forcing the changes rippling under his skin to stop. He couldn't shift here. He dug his phone out of his pocket without opening his eyes, then shoved it at the bed. "Warn everyone. Tell them to hunker down at my cabin."

"Yes, sir." Micah spoke quietly on the phone, working through the pack as Otis reined in his temper. His mind raced, his thoughts scattering so fast that he couldn't keep up, and his fangs kept punching through his bottom lip.

"Shit," he muttered again, gesturing for his phone back. Micah hung up and handed it over.

Otis dialed by memory, the numbers blurring under his thumb. The three rings before she picked up were the longest seconds of his life.

"Get back to my cabin," he told Bree without greeting. "Boiling River's not safe."

She snorted, the sound crackling down the line.

"That's not news, Pascale. My apartment burned down yesterday."

"Will you just—" he broke off, sucking in a deep breath. "Don't fight me on this, okay? Do as you're told."

He knew as soon as the words came out they were the worst possible thing he could say. Micah cringed visibly on the bed, his mouth stretching into a grimace.

Bree's voice was murderous when she spoke.

"You are not my alpha, Pascale. You have no gods-damned right to boss me around."

Otis threw up his spare hand. "Are you hearing me? It's dangerous! Get back where it's safe."

"I'll find my own shelter." He opened his mouth to argue, but the phone beeped in his ear, the call ended. Otis cursed loudly, tossing the phone back on the bed and waving at Micah to carry on his job.

He couldn't do it. Couldn't protect an entire pack of werewolves, run a radio station, and babysit his mate who wouldn't listen to reason.

Bree Mendez didn't want to be his problem. She was on her own.

* * *

Otis held his ground for approximately five minutes before his chest caved in. The thought of her out there, at risk and maybe a target... Otis rubbed at his throat as he dialed Zacharias. Evening drew in through the hospital window, the sky bruising and darkening as the sun sank behind the mountains.

"Come on, Otis, I'm not even late," the vampire growled in his ear. "I don't start work for another twenty minutes."

"I need you to do something for me. It's important."

"Alright," Zacharias said at once. "What do you need?"

"You know Claire's friend, Bree Mendez?" Otis heard the vampire's long-suffering sigh.

"Rather more than I'd like."

"I need you to find her and stay with her. Right now. No matter what she says. The pack's under attack, and she's a target too."

"It's done." Otis closed his eyes, the knot easing in his chest. Zacharias was supernatural, an immortal no less. He'd be more than a match for whatever was stalking Boiling River. "But, man... why doesn't she come to you?"

"Ask her that," Otis ground out. "Maybe she'll have a decent answer for you."

Zacharias snorted. "I doubt it. Bree doesn't do feelings."

Otis hung up, a million bitter words lined up on his tongue. He knew that fact better than anyone.

She could be an ass if she wanted. She could refuse his protection. It was important to him that she felt respected and heard.

Zacharias, however, had no such reservations for his girl's noisy friend.

Chapter 9

"Alright." Zacharias clapped his hands together, standing over his sofa. Bree, Claire and Olivia were sprawled on the cushions, blinking up at the vampire. His crimson eyes kept darting to the exit. "Netflix is up and loaded. I've ordered Thai food, which Claire tells me is somehow superior. You all have free access to the pool and other facilities."

Bree leaned over to stage-whisper in Claire's ear.

"What's wrong with him? Why is he in dad-mode? Are you pregnant?"

Claire shook her head slowly, frowning up at her boyfriend. There was a pink dishcloth tossed over his shoulder.

"Zacharias, honey." She pushed off the sofa, the buckle of her painter's overalls snagging in Olivia's hair. "Why are you trying to babysit us? Are you low on blood?"

"No, I am not thirsty." The vampire pinched the bridge of his narrow nose. Dark tendrils of his long hair had escaped their tie and hung around his face, much like Bree's. She tipped her head back and stared at the ceiling, wondering if Claire had noticed she was dating her best friend's male lookalike.

Zacharias ranted, his voice rising in pitch as he pointed out the various entertainment options for the evening. Bree finally broke, clapping her hands on her thighs when he suggested a jigsaw puzzle.

"Well, this has been fun, Z, but I've gotta head out."

Yes, she'd come to the vampire's underground apartment as soon as Otis called warning about an attack. She'd figured Zacharias was strong, an immortal vampire, and though she rankled him on a weekly basis, she figured he'd protect her, if only for Claire's sake.

Bree hadn't banked on Zacharias having some kind of meltdown. She wasn't socially equipped for this.

"You can't leave." The vampire's voice was strained, his face clearly telling her that he dearly wished she could. "Otis asked me to watch you."

Bree balled her hands into fists. "I'm not a child."

"But you are in danger."

"That's why I came here!"

Zacharias threw his arms wide. "Then why leave now, you insufferable woman?"

"Because I don't want to do jigsaw puzzles! I'm not a thousand years old, you lunatic!"

Claire watched them bicker, her red head swinging between them like she was watching a tennis match. Olivia reached over and grabbed her sleeve, tugging her back down onto the sofa, and the two of them began to flick through movies. Bree gave as good as she got, yelling at Zacharias and throttling the air, but it was Otis she truly wanted to kill.

"Enough," Zacharias snapped, holding up a palm. He layered his glamor into the command, his voice melodic.

Bree's mouth clicked shut. She poured every ounce of her loathing into her eyes.

"Yes, you hate me, etcetera, etcetera." He thrust a phone at her. "Take it up with Otis. I'm out." He stalked across the stone floor, Claire's head turning to watch him go. He made a beeline straight to the collection of houseplants displayed on shelves against one wall, snatching up a spray bottle and misting the leaves.

"Here we go," Claire muttered as the vampire started cursing under his breath. "I'll get him some blood."

Maybe she should feel bad, but Bree couldn't find it in herself to care about Zacharias and his rage-misting. She pulled up Otis' phone number and pressed call, squeezing the phone so hard it cracked.

"What?" He barked out, apparently just as pissed off as everyone else. Only Olivia was serene, settling in for her favorite slasher movie. "Has something happened?"

"Oh, you know." Bree kicked at a pillar. "Just being forcibly babysat by a vampire."

"I'm not sorry."

Bree's fingers flexed. "Not yet, anyway."

"It's for your safety. You could have come here."

"Maybe I'll call Danny," Bree spat out, then immediately wished she could take it back. Down the line, Otis fell silent.

"If you like," he said after a long pause. His voice was robotic. "You'll be safe with him."

"Otis—"

"Goodnight, Bree." The line went dead. She dug the corner of the phone into her forehead.

"All settled?" Zacharias asked, striding past her to the kitchen.

"No."

"Oh, well. You'll live."

Bree turned on her heel and marched past Claire's nervous smile, tugging her shirt over her head and tossing it to the tiles. She needed to swim.

If she didn't burn some of this anger off, none of them would leave the vampire's stupid evil bunker alive.

* * *

"Don't say it," Bree blurted when the cabin door swung open. Otis was not pleased to see her. He leaned out of his doorway, scanning the porch behind her.

"Where's Zacharias?"

"Distracted."

"By what?"

"A movie."

"A *movie*—"

Bree put up her hands. "I put on Titanic."

Otis let out a slow breath, shaking his head. Behind him, his cabin was noisy and filled with light.

"Low blow."

"Yeah, I know. But I couldn't stay there."

Otis' mouth twisted, his fingers drumming on the door frame.

"You could have called. I would have come and fetched you."

All the bitterness surged back up Bree's throat. She was a grown woman, damn it, not a naughty child, and it was hardly a special occasion to have a dangerous creature in town. Boiling River had so many things going bump in the night, the town newspaper kept running out of ink.

"I don't need an *escort*—"

"Alright." He cut her off, shaking his head. "Alright, Bree. I get the picture." His words were tired, like she drained him just by being near, but Otis stepped back and waved an arm through the doorway. Bree shuffled inside, her skin prickling with the weight of a dozen predators' eyes.

The werewolves lounged on every surface, their bare limbs gleaming in the firelight. They all wore shorts and t-shirts or vests. The only exception was a pale, lean guy with curly reddish-brown hair and quick, green eyes. He watched her from the kitchen doorway, his shoulder propped against the frame, his long limbs clad in a sweater and jeans.

"Gentlemen." Bree nodded at the wolves. The old guy Pedro saluted back— a longtime regular at the bar.

"Why's she here—" a young guy started to ask, but Otis cuffed him up the back of the head as he walked past. The young wolf smirked over his shoulder at the alpha. "You got a girlfriend, boss?"

"Nope." Otis strode into his kitchen, digging for two beers in the fridge. He came back into the cramped living space, holding a bottle out to Bree. "This is Breanna Mendez. She's under our protection."

"You in trouble, Bree?" Pedro asked, his bristly face creased with concern. She shrugged and forced a smile.

"No more than usual."

Pedro chuckled. "I'll take that as a yes."

It took a while, but the werewolves settled back down, easing back against their sofa cushions and bean bags. One guy stood up, walked to the corner and stripped, before shifting and curling up on the rug.

"That looks pretty nice," Bree murmured when Otis came to

61

stand by her shoulder. The firelight glinted in the wolf's glossy dark fur.

"It hurts." The admission took her by surprise. The wolves were so macho, so freaking gung-ho about their pack, she'd never heard one mention a drawback.

"The whole time you're a wolf?" She hated that thought. "Or just while you're shifting?"

"Just the shift." Otis cracked a lazy smile. He'd forgiven her, then. The knot in her stomach loosened. "I get vertigo sometimes."

Bree snorted. "No, thanks."

"Tell me about it."

Her head dropped, resting on his shoulder. Otis said nothing, and even though curious sets of eyes flicked her way, she stayed with her forehead leaned against his toned shoulder.

The movement was automatic. The act of an impulse. But now she was here, she didn't want to move away.

"I should have come earlier."

Otis grunted. "Why didn't you?" He swigged from his beer while he waited for her to answer.

"I'm my own person," she said at last, measuring her words. "I make my own decisions, good or bad. That's who I am."

Otis nudged her cheek. The fabric of his shirt was soft. It smelled like washing powder and eucalyptus.

"Maybe I'll ask nicely next time."

"I don't believe you, somehow."

They smirked at the fire together.

It wasn't so bad, now she was here. Maybe she could try not to fight every step of the way.

* * *

One by one, the werewolves dropped to sleep. All except the sharp-eyed man in jeans and Otis, who brewed pot after pot of coffee, clutching his mug in a broad hand.

"You can take a break," the guy said at last, coming to crouch where Bree and Otis were slumped against the wall. "I'll keep watch."

Bree braced for Otis to turn the offer down. Instead he sighed and cracked his neck before pushing to his feet, reaching down to pull Bree up too.

"Wake me in an hour," was all he said. "Sooner if you get tired."

The guy nodded, striding to the counter and hopping up, bending his legs and resting his chin on his knees. His eyes fixed on the shadows outside the window, his senses better than Bree would ever know.

"Come on," Otis murmured, still holding Bree's hand. He tugged her towards his bedroom.

"You told them I'm not your girlfriend," she hissed, tripping as they passed through the doorway. He pushed the door closed behind them, leaving a two-inch gap for firelight to shine through. The room was exactly as she'd left it this morning, down to the messily made bed and the alarm clock tipped down onto its face.

Otis chuckled, the sound husky. "Since when did you care what people think?"

True. Bree nodded, wrapping her arms around her waist as she approached the bed. The only bed. As if reading her mind, Otis nudged her closer, his palm warm on the small of her back.

"Go on. I'll take the floor."

"Otis—"

"It's fine. Go on."

His tone was gentle, but it left no room for argument. For the first time, Bree understood why the pack of wolves would follow their alpha to the ends of the earth. He was commanding, sure of himself, yet gentle and considerate too. Otis did no harm, but he took no shit.

Bree liked that about him.

Kicking her boots off onto the rug, Bree crawled onto the mattress, jeans and all. Last night, she'd slept in Otis' clothes, but that felt far too intimate an act with the twelve witnesses sprawled out there in the cabin. If something happened, if something came, she wanted to be ready. She'd be no one's damsel in distress.

Otis grabbed a pillow and tossed it onto the floor next to the bed. Bree watched him, sat up against the headboard with his blankets pooled around her lap as he dug in his closet for a spare throw.

When he came up empty handed, all his supplies already handed out to the wolves, Otis said nothing. Not a word of complaint. He simply smiled at her, his amber eyes bright in the moonlight, and dropped to the floor, stretching out on the bare rug.

Bree shuffled down until she lay flat, tugging the covers up to her chin. Nights were cold in the desert, and the glass window panes were already steamed over from the icy night.

She bit her lip. "Otis."

He grunted at her whisper.

"Do you want to come up here?"

A floorboard creaked. He paused, silent, barely breathing, then rolled over, getting comfortable again.

"I'm good. Go to sleep, Bree."

She huffed. Her hand patted down the side of the mattress, down the wooden bed frame, reaching into the darkness until her fingertips brushed a warm cotton t-shirt. Bree grasped a handful of fabric, giving a shake.

"Don't be noble. Come up here."

"Bree."

"It's cold tonight."

"I run hot."

"The floor's hard."

"It's good for the spine."

"Otis Pascale, I swear to the gods," Bree hissed. "Get your ass in this bed."

A series of scrapes and thumps echoed in the shadows, the dark outline of Otis' form lurching above the bed as he pushed to his feet. Bree watched him from the pillow, her body tingling in a way she didn't understand, and only loosed a breath when he wandered away, rounding the foot of the bed.

"No complaining if I snore, now."

The mattress dipped under his weight. Bree steeled herself and rolled over, their faces lining up on the pillows so his breath washed over her cheeks. The waistband of her jeans was twisted, the button digging into her stomach, and she was already way too hot.

"Bree," Otis murmured. The thin column of firelight slanted over his face, lighting up one amber eye. She reached out, impossibly slow, and ran a fingertip over his beard.

Otis sighed, his eyes drifting shut, locking away that amber glow.

"Bree," he said again, a warning note in his voice. His beard was so soft against the pad of her finger. Glossy, thick and well-trimmed. She traced the edge of his jaw all the way to his chin, dipping her fingertip into the cleft hidden under the hair.

"What?" she asked, distracted. He smelled really freaking good.

A warm grip wrapped around her wrist.

"Don't play with me, Mendez." He tugged her away and placed her hand back on her pillow. "Don't start something you can't finish."

Chapter 10

*H*e hadn't meant it to sound like a challenge. If Otis knew Bree Mendez at all - and he flattered himself that he knew her better than anyone, that he understood her better than she did herself—it was that she couldn't leave a challenge unmet. It was pathological.

Sure enough, Bree shifted closer on the mattress, the covers sliding over her body. It was torture, having her this near. Having her scent envelop him—dark cherries and leather and something else. Something spicy.

"Who says I can't finish it?" She cocked her head, the motion visible in the gloom even without his wolf eyes. Her hand slid towards him again, reaching across the pillow, and Otis stilled it with a flattened palm.

This was the problem with Bree. She was all impulse; all action. The gods knew Otis loved her fiery spirit, but that did not mean he'd line up to be collateral damage.

"Really?" Otis asked, his voice light. "Does that mean you're ready to talk about us?"

The silence that rang through the bedroom was enough to set his teeth on edge.

"That's not fair," Bree choked out. Otis shut his eyes. If Bree had her way, she'd run from this their whole lives.

"No." His voice was harder than he intended. She flinched back against the pillow. "What's not fair is being chosen for a mate who can't commit. Now that is a cosmic joke." He let go of her hand and rolled over, glaring out the bedroom window, his body as tense as a board.

After a while, he heard her turn over too, the covers whispering. Her breath slowed as she pretended to sleep.

She couldn't fool him. Even her deep, slow breaths couldn't distract from her racing heart. He'd frightened her, either with his harsh tone or with the terrifying implications of his words. He'd almost forced her to confront the one thing Bree was most scared of—the fact that her fate had been chosen for her.

Otis squeezed his eyes shut, regret already throbbing sickly in his chest.

He shouldn't have done that. Shouldn't have cornered her like that. But the way she reached for him, her voice light and teasing, like it meant nothing. Like he would be just another fling…

Otis threw back the covers and stood up without a word. He couldn't be here anymore. He'd take over the watch, and Micah could get some sleep, and he'd get far enough away from Bree to breathe again.

* * *

"Are you sure?" Micah's voice was hushed. "I could stay up. Keep you company."

"I'm sure." Otis avoided his beta's eyes as he stepped past to the front door. He'd keep watch on the porch, away from the muggy air in the living room, heated by twelve warm bodies—away from prying eyes and straining ears.

Damn. Werewolves never got a moment alone.

The icy night air slapped his cheeks as he pushed the door open. The firelight spilled outside, flickering across the baked dirt, and Otis stared into the deepest shadows to let his eyes adjust.

Resting. He was resting. Getting a moment's reprieve from the others, from Bree. He was not sulking, or hiding away like a moody teenager, no matter what he whispered in his own head.

"Shit," Otis said, scuffing his boot over the porch. A fine layer of dirt crunched against the worn floorboards. He was doing this all wrong, somehow. The pack; the radio station; his mate. Otis tried so hard to do right by everyone, but every day he seemed to find a new way to mess this all up.

He scratched his beard, the hairs cropped close to his chin. Maybe he was trying too hard. Zacharias and Claire didn't have to work to like each other—not once they got to know each other, at least. And if he eased off on the pack, let a few things slide, would they really all leave for another alpha?

And if they did, would that be the worst thing in the world?

A flare of light caught Otis' eye, sparking in the distance. It arced into the air, sailing towards the cabin: a glass bottle stuffed with a lit rag.

He didn't think. He acted on instinct, lunging forward and batting away the bottle with a bare, open palm. The heat scorched his hand, but the bottle whipped sideways into the desert before smashing against a large cactus. Fire burst and spread, swarming over the giant plant, and casting long shadows which danced over the dirt.

"Micah!" Otis yelled, the name warping as his face transformed into a muzzle. He dropped to all fours, his clothes shredding off his back, and snarled, leaping off the porch.

They were here. Whoever kept threatening Bree and his wolves.

His paws pounded over the cracked earth, rattlesnakes hissing and flinching out of his path. Cacti and boulders loomed up on all sides, the desert a maze of shadows, but Otis sniffed and followed the scent. It was faint, barely there, but alien enough out in the wastes that he couldn't miss it.

Tobacco and bacon grease. Cheap soap and diesel oil. Recognition tickled at the back of Otis' head.

The scent grew stronger as he streaked through the valley, his footsteps sure and his limbs strong. It had been a long time since he hunted like this—too long. His wolf was savage, barely restrained, and it would take everything in him not to rip this person to shreds—

Glass shattered back at the cabin. There was a distant thump and a yell. Otis snarled, his head jerking back toward the cabin as his feet kept carrying him forwards. His instincts warred—to hunt and kill, and to protect his mate and pack.

Later, he'd be ashamed of the long seconds between hearing that crash and spinning around. His heart thundered in his chest as he pounded back toward his home, that scent still fresh in his nose.

He found Bree on the porch, her body drowned in one of his sweaters and her eyes wide as she watched for him. Jason stood by her side, his shoulders tense and vibrating, and the others gathered around the cactus, throwing buckets of water on the fire. It was a huge task—the cactus was the size of a small oak tree—but Micah directed them to the worst of the flames.

The family of owls which nested in the cactus fluttered onto his roof, their feathers singed.

"Otis?" Bree called as he trotted toward the porch. He shifted on the edge of the shadows.

"Lucky for you," he called back. "For future reference, please don't assume every wolf you see is me."

He could practically hear her eye roll from here. Otis grinned, waving for Jason's better eyes. The pup bent and picked up a stack of fresh clothes, tossing them into the darkness.

"Another outfit bites the dust?" Her words were light, but the relief was stark on Bree's face when he stepped into the light.

Otis dipped his chin at the pile of shredded fabric.

"Those were my favorite jeans."

"I'm so sorry for your loss."

They smirked at each other, something throbbing in Otis' chest, until Jason's cleared throat brought him back to earth.

"Boss. Shall I…?" He jerked his head at the fire.

"Yes. Yeah." Otis flapped a hand. "Go and help." Jason nodded, visibly relieved, and jumped down the porch steps, taking off at a run for the cactus.

"Why don't they shift?" Bree asked. "I thought your wolves were stronger?"

Otis snorted. "Can't hold buckets of water with paws." Silence stretched between them, not as strained as before, but his words were still awkward when he spoke again. "I heard breaking glass…?"

Bree bit her lip. "I dropped a beer bottle. I'm sorry. I'll clean it up, I swear—"

Otis waved her words away. "Leave it, Mendez. You've cleaned up plenty of broken glasses after us." The porch steps groaned under his weight, and he joined her, staring out at the desert valley. It was dark, with only stars blanketing the night sky. No dancing aurora of magic tonight; no pulsing lights of space ships.

Only glittering galaxies overhead, and the odd flying Molotov cocktail.

"Do you know who it was?"

Otis hummed. "I have a theory. But I need to be sure. Can't go throwing accusations around like confetti."

Bree nudged him with her shoulder. "That doesn't stop most people."

"Guess I'm a special snowflake."

"Guess so."

He darted a look at her out of the corner of his eye. She'd picked out his ugliest sweater—the pride of his closet. A knitted monstrosity that looked like a basket of yarn balls fought in a bag and all lost. The colors clashed, the stitches sagged then bunched in turn, and loose threads dangled from each elbow.

It was a gift from Mabel, the town banshee and Claire's little old lady neighbor. Otis couldn't love it more if he tried.

"Nice sweater."

"Thank you."

"You have great taste."

"So I do." Bree sighed and turned to him. "When I don't fight myself, anyway."

She could mean anything by that. He couldn't let himself hope—it would only hurt more on the other side.

"What do you mean?" Otis asked, as casually as he could

manage. Out of the corner of his eye, he watched Bree step closer.

Her hand was warm as it cupped his elbow, his upper half bare except for a sage green t-shirt. Her touch slid up his arm, her fingertips dipping into the grooves of his muscles then squeezing his shoulder bones.

"Bree," Otis ground out. His mouth was dry. "I told you. Don't play with me."

"Maybe I'm not playing." Her hand slid to his neck. She rocked up on her toes and scratched at his hair. If he were in his wolf form, he'd have whimpered and melted into a puddle at her feet. As it was…

"Stop." He caught her hand and pulled it away. "Wait a minute. Tell me what you're thinking."

"I'm thinking about you," she snapped. Only Bree could confess her feelings like they were a nuisance. His mouth quirked.

"Oh yeah? Which parts of me?"

She rolled her eyes. He flipped her hand over in his grip and started kneading her palm. Her thumb joint was stiff, so he focused there, rubbing small circles into the muscle.

"I can't… promise anything."

He already knew that.

"Can you promise to try? To give it a fair chance?"

Her whisper was almost lost among the werewolves' distant shouts.

"Yes. I can do that."

Otis couldn't wait any longer. He'd dreamed of this moment for months—years, even. Ever since he'd first walked into the Silver Bullet and his heart had seized at the sight of the bartender. He pulled lightly on her hand, tugging Bree to step forward until they were chest to chest. On the dusty porch, her socked feet were toe-to-toe with his bare ones.

He skimmed his thumb along her jaw. When her eyes fluttered closed, his heart stuttered, missing a beat.

This was happening. Really happening. Otis dipped his head and paused, their mouths a hair's breadth apart.

"Are you sure—"

Bree surged up, closing the gap between them and sealing her mouth to his. Her fingers gripped his t-shirt, holding him in place, and Otis kissed her back like his life depended on it. Wolf whistles echoed over from the pack, but he ignored them, too wrapped up in the feel and taste of Bree to even bother flipping them off.

He needn't worry. Bree dragged a hand off his chest and did it for him.

The whistles grew louder, breaking into laughter, and Bree's mouth curved against his in a smile.

She wanted this. At last, she wanted him.

His mate.

Chapter 11

*D*ating a werewolf was not what Bree expected.

She didn't know what she'd imagined. Dog hair on the furniture? Twice daily walks? Constant yips for attention? Whatever she'd thought, she was wrong. So, so wrong.

Otis didn't ask her out for three days after the fire. Oh, he texted her, several times a day, and called every night as Bree curled up on Zacharias' sofa. The vampire had looked on the verge of despair when Bree knocked on his door with what was left of her belongings, but Claire's freckled, smiling face popped up over his shoulder.

"Of course you can stay!" her friend sang, elbowing her boyfriend in the gut. "There's plenty of room, right Zacharias?"

"It would appear so."

Otis had offered his cabin, too, but he seemed to understand when she said she needed space. He'd walked her into town, his warm hand hovering near her back, his footsteps lighter than she'd ever seen.

They were doing this. Really doing this. But the only way she'd keep her head was if they moved at her pace. That meant no rushing to move in together, no matter that she was technically homeless. And no spending every waking moment in each other's presence.

When Bree made that rule, she hadn't accounted for how much she'd think of him.

Admitting to herself and to Otis that she liked him—it was like opening a floodgate. All the secret stirrings she'd felt in her gut over the years, all the nights she'd dreamed about him then pretended it never happened—they all came crashing down on her in one huge wave. The enormity of her crush on Otis Pascale swallowed her whole; sent her spinning into its depths.

Too late to back out now. She'd done it. Admitted how she felt. All Bree was left with now was a constant, nagging need to speak with him. To see him, to press her nose against his collarbone and inhale.

To kiss him again.

When her phone buzzed on their third day apart, vibrating against Zacharias' coffee table, Bree moved so fast she practically blurred. She accepted the call, pressing the phone against her ear, and stuck up her middle finger at Zacharias snickering on the other sofa.

"Hello?"

"Still taking my calls, then." His voice was warm. Teasing, but with an undercurrent of worry. Like he'd thought she might change her mind already. Run away from everything brewing between them, and make off for the hills.

It was fair enough for him to worry. She'd half wondered that herself, but when she examined that option, something clenched in her gut.

The thought of leaving him now, of setting out into the world with a piece of herself left behind in Boiling River... it hurt.

Still. No need to stroke his ego.

"I didn't look at the caller ID. Thought it was Charlton. My bad."

Otis' laugh was soft. Intimate. Like he was curled around her, whispering in her ear.

"What are you doing tomorrow?"

Bree sucked her teeth, staring down at her feet. Her toes scrunched against the stone tiles, warmed by a pair of fluffy socks borrowed from Claire.

She had nothing. Barely any possessions, and no money to replace her burned things. Not shifts at the Silver Bullet. No job, no home, no plan.

"Oh, you know." Bree grimaced. "Sorting my life out... somehow."

Otis hummed. Just that sound was enough to soothe the panic gnawing at her chest.

"Want some help? I'm a respected man, you know. Maybe I could help you find work."

Bree couldn't keep the goofy smile from her face. Claire whispered something in her boyfriend's ear, the two of them curled up on the sofa, and Zacharias tipped back his head and roared with laughter. Bree threw a pillow at his face, her mouth still stretched in a grin.

"Since when are you respected?"

"By everyone else, Bree. Not you."

"Just checking."

She screwed her eyes shut, warring between the butterflies in her stomach and the fear squeezing her heart. Everyone left eventually. Her parents hadn't called her in months. If she let

Otis in, truly let him in, and then something drove him away too…

"Meet me in the town square at midday. Don't be late."

"I wouldn't dare. Give Zacharias my undying love."

Bree snorted and tossed the phone to the sofa. Otis and Zacharias had an unlikely bromance, the two men complete opposites. Zacharias was stiff and formal where Otis was all laid-back ease. The vampire was fiercely private where the werewolf was a wide open book.

She didn't pass the message along. She'd only get another pillow to the face.

* * *

The town library was cool when Bree ducked her head inside, the air laced with the scent of old paper. The lights on the walls were off, the bulbs dark in their sconces, and long shadows stretched across the parquet tiles. Bree stepped through the doorway, something banging in the depths of the cavernous room.

"Olivia?" she called, her voice bouncing off the high ceiling.

"Hey."

Bree jumped, her hand smacking against her chest. Olivia stood between the stacks on the left, a hardback book clutched in one hand. Her silvery blonde hair looked eerie in the gloom. Bree forced out a breath.

"Why are you creeping around in the dark?"

Olivia shrugged, pushing her glasses up her nose before squinting at the book's spine. Bree strode to the lighting panel and smacked the lights on. The bulbs flickered, slow to come to life, but gradually the library was filled with a warm glow.

"Liv..." Bree chewed on her bottom lip. Olivia wore the same clothes she'd been dressed in for movie night last night. She wore the same chunky pink cardigan and navy blue skirt, the same wrinkled white t-shirt underneath. "Did you go home last night?"

Olivia slid the book onto its shelf.

"You're up early." Her voice was dull. Robotic.

"Just getting away from the vampire for a few hours. Liv... what's going on?"

Bree wasn't blind. Olivia hadn't been well for months, her usually bright complexion growing pale and wan. Though her friend had never been the life of the party, Olivia had retreated inside herself, burying herself in her work in the library. Claire had noticed it too, murmuring about it to Bree one night, but what could they do? They asked, but Olivia wasn't telling.

Whenever they spoke, Bree got the feeling she was only half listening. That something or someone else was whispering in her other ear.

"I'm just tired." Olivia gave her a shaky smile, reaching for another book on the trolley. Half her fingernails were painted pale blue, the others bare like she'd forgotten mid-task.

"Of course you're tired. You haven't slept." This wasn't the first all-nighter Olivia had pulled. These days, she spent more time drifting through the stacks than in her own bed.

Well, enough. Bree had plenty of flaws, and conveniently, one of them was bossiness. She marched over to her friend, grasping her by the elbow and tugging her to the door.

"Come on. We're getting coffee."

"I thought you were broke."

"Fine, you're getting coffee. I'm going to watch you drink it like a creep." Olivia blinked in the sunshine when they stepped outside, raising an arm to shield her eyes. "Yep," Bree continued, dragging her friend across the town square. Two vultures perched on a bench, scrapping for space. "It's bright out when you hide from the sun like a troll. Come on, we're getting some food in you, too."

There weren't many places open this early. Boiling River was not a town of morning people, instead boasting a roaring trade in novelty cocktails and late night kebabs. But one cafe had chairs and tables set outside, its awning pulled up and the scent of fresh bread floating through the door.

"Sit." Bree nudged Olivia into a chair. Damn. She'd been around the wolves too much, but Olivia sat without complaint, even offering her a watery smile. "What do you feel like?"

"Coffee." Olivia bit her lip. "And cake."

"Done." Bree marched inside to place the order, getting the same for herself. She'd scrape together the cash from the bottom of her wallet and deal with the consequences later. Something wasn't right.

Bree watched through the glass display windows as Olivia slumped in her chair, like a puppet with cut strings. A pale finger came up to scratch at the metal table.

Bree frowned. Olivia's lips were moving. Her friend was talking to herself.

"Who's here?" Olivia jumped as Bree stood in the cafe doorway, hands on hips. "Who are you talking to?"

For a moment, she thought she'd cracked it. That Olivia would finally talk. Her friend paused, her mouth slightly open. Then her mouth stretched into a fake smile, a laugh bursting between her lips.

"What are you talking about? No one's here."

Bree stared at her for a moment longer, watching her squirm.

Then she nodded, set her jaw, and strode back inside to fetch their order.

Olivia would tell her when she was ready. But this wasn't over.

Chapter 12

⚜

*O*tis had longed for this date for years. *Years.* He'd pictured it endlessly, dreaming up different activities and restaurants and conversations. Trying to figure out that perfect formula which would make Bree forget her long-running grudge and accept him as her mate.

He'd figured there would be flowers. Music. A starry night sky and free-flowing drinks to smooth over their rough edges.

The reality couldn't be more different.

Otis jogged into the town square as the library clock tower struck midday. He'd wanted to be early—he planned to sit and wait on one of the town benches and give Bree an I-told-you-so smirk as she arrived. But rushing through a full day's worth of work at Supernatural Airwaves in one morning had taken its toll. He was harried, barely getting through his most important tasks, and at one point Angie had to cut him off the coffee supply.

Essential forms were lost.

Tubs of paper clips were knocked flying.

The keys to the radio station were found in the staff room refrigerator.

Otis was never like this. He was laid back to a fault, taking his sweet time to do things properly and not letting stress cut through his thick skin. In his calmness, he got the job done, and he did it well, no matter what Zacharias might say.

Today was different.

He was on edge, his wolf instincts screaming at him to get-this-freaking-right, or else prepare for a lonely life of misery. And it wasn't just Bree that set his senses tingling. The whole gods-damned town felt off as he jogged through the streets, the seconds counting down before the biggest date of his life. New security cameras hung above doorways, freshly installed, with their bug-eyed lenses pointing down at the sidewalk. Curtains twitched as he ran past; cars locked from the inside.

Boiling River was frightened.

Otis careened into the town square on the clock tower's third strike. Bree sat on one of the benches by the statue of a giant, the stone figure looming above the paving slabs. A vulture with bulging, watery eyes and a bent feather on its head was perched beside her, pecking at the strands of her hair as they danced in the warm breeze.

She didn't even notice. Bree sat with her elbows leaned on her knees, scowling at the pale stone slabs, and didn't glance up until the third time Otis said her name.

She blinked at him, confusion creasing her brow, before she visibly remembered their date.

Not a good start.

"Hi." Otis shoved his hands in his jean pockets. "Everything okay?"

Bree's frown deepened. "Of course. Why wouldn't it be?"

Several reasons lined up on the tip of Otis' tongue, starting with her burned down apartment and lost job and ending with the grumpy set to her mouth.

"No reason." Otis smiled, swiping his forearm over his forehead. He'd run straight here from the radio station, the hot desert sun beating down against his neck. Did he smell? Were there giant sweat stains under his arms?

Gods, this was a disaster. He hadn't bombed a first date like this since he was a gawky teenager.

"So, where should we start?" he asked when Bree said nothing for a full twenty seconds. He waved around the town square. "We could see who's hiring? Or we could check the community boards for rentals—"

"I don't want to do those things."

"Oooh-kay."

This was her idea. She wanted to sort her life out; he wasn't the one without a job or home. Otis stared down at Bree for a long moment, tapping his leg, then cursed and sat beside her on the bench.

"What's going on, Bree?" His voice was flat. Dead. They hadn't even made it two minutes. Hadn't left the freaking town square.

She shrugged, pulling her knees up and wrapping her arms around her legs. Her jeans were frayed at the hem.

Otis waited for her to say something. Anything. But she was silent.

Okay. Alright. He'd—he'd tried. He couldn't force her to give him a proper chance, and though it killed him, he couldn't chase her forever.

He clapped his hands on his thighs.

"Alright, Bree. Call me if you need anything."

Chapter 12

Otis made to stand up, disappointment sour in his mouth. He'd screwed up his whole day's work for this? But as he pushed upright, a hand shot out and grabbed his elbow.

"Wait a second. Just—don't go."

Otis settled back down. He'd give her a minute. Maybe two. ... Maybe ten.

"It's all just..." Bree trailed off, then sucked in a shaky breath. "It's all so big. My job and my apartment and my bank and Olivia and now this thing with you. I know I need to fix all these problems, but I don't know where to start. And when I try, it's like I freeze up."

Otis hummed. She was talking. Confiding in him. This was progress, even though he only followed half of it.

"What do you want to do?"

Bree squinted up at the statue, her mouth twisting.

Then: "Play pool."

A grin spread across his face. Hell yeah, they could play pool. But first...

"I'll make you a deal. We walk around the square. Find three job applications for you to fill out. Then we play pool, and I buy us both burgers, too."

Bree's stomach growled audibly. She shot him a wry smile. "You drive a mean bargain."

Otis shrugged. "I've had lots of practice."

"Right. I bet the wolves are much harder work than me."

Otis snorted. "Don't be so sure."

He pushed to his feet before the smile could fade from her face. He knew moods like this well. The trick was to stay in motion, to not give those clammy fears the chance to catch up to you.

"Come on." He held out a hand. "Let's go earn your burger."

"And fries?"

Her fingers were small in his. He tugged her to her feet.

"What am I, a monster? Of course fries."

* * *

When Bree Mendez was in a good mood, there was no brighter force of nature. Otis watched, spellbound, as she leaned over the pool table, glancing up to give him a wink. Their empty plates were stacked nearby, their half-drunk milkshakes sweating on the diner table, and every time Bree looked his way, Otis just about had a heart attack.

So this was what it was like to be with his mate.

When she wanted him around. When she was happy to see him. When she tossed back her head and laughed at his jokes; when she darted him glances from beneath her lashes, her lips curled with promise.

Gods. It was only 3pm. He'd never make it through the day.

"Yes!" Bree punched the air as her ball clicked into the pocket. "Suck it, Fido!"

Otis grinned, pushing off his stool and grabbing his cue.

"Don't get cocky, Mendez."

It had been like this for hours. After that bumpy start, Bree had trailed around the local businesses with her mouth pressed in a firm line. But with each place that was hiring, she turned on the charm, laughing and chatting easily like there was nowhere she'd rather be.

She'd had two offers already, from the emporium and Hex Mex. With each new application she filled out, the tension eased in her jaw.

Bree would be fine. She was stronger than she thought. Hell, even the owner of this diner looked ready to beg her to stay.

She was natural. That was it. She was funny and hard working, and she treated customers like they were old friends. The Boiling River tourists loved her—in the Silver Bullet, they often lined up to get pictures with her for social media.

Otis knew Bree thought she was a failure. He also knew she was dead wrong.

"Watch how it's done." He potted the ball with a firm stroke, then grinned up at Bree. "Are you impressed yet, Mendez?"

She rolled her eyes, but she couldn't hide the smile tugging at her mouth.

"Go jump in the river, Pascale."

He splayed a hand over his chest. "So harsh."

The air was different between them today. Oh, it was always fraught, the molecules practically vibrating with tension. But this time, it was a good kind of tension—like the air was shivering with anticipation.

He knew the feeling. Otis opened his mouth, ready to throw it all on the table and ask her back to his cabin. Not to bed, necessarily—though the gods knew he wouldn't say no—but to be alone together. Finally.

Before he could speak, a crash sounded outside the diner, a faint scream echoing in from the street. Otis took off running, his mind wiped blank by instinct as he sprinted toward that scream.

He burst out of the doorway and smelled blood. A growl vibrated in his chest, and his fangs punctured his bottom lip.

Not now—not yet. Otis reined in the shift, running on foot towards the crowd gathering a short way down the street. This block lay on the outskirts of town, the street spilling into the wide open desert. The buildings were mostly townhouses and small businesses; there was a nursing home, a florist, and a vintage mask-maker.

The crowd gathered two houses down from the nursing home, around something slumped on the sidewalk. Something tickled at the back of Otis' mind, and he ran faster, his legs pumping.

He knew that scent. Diesel oil and bacon grease. And he knew the body slumped on the ground.

"Pedro!" Otis shouldered his way to the older wolf's side, dropping to his knees. Pedro blinked up at him, dazed, blood trickling from a deep gash above his ear. Otis tugged his t-shirt over his head, balling it up and pressing it against the wound. He yelled for someone to call 911 before turning back to his wolf.

Pedro's eyes were unfocused. A bouquet of fresh daisies were held loosely in his grip.

"What happened?" Pedro didn't answer. He showed no signs of hearing him. Otis looked around the crowd instead, pouring every inch of his alpha's command into his words. "Someone tell me. What happened?"

A pixie-like teenage girl stepped forward, her lip trembling, compelled by his order.

"Someone hit him. They came up behind him and ran away." "Did you see it?"

The girl nodded. She pointed to the florist across the street. "I was in there. But they wore a hood. I didn't see their face."

Otis swallowed back a snarl. It wasn't this girl's fault, no matter how he wanted to tear someone's head off. A hand landed on his shoulder, squeezing gently, and Bree's scent floated around him.

His temper eased slightly.

"Was it human?" he bit out. The girl nodded frantically. "A man?"

"I think so."

Coupled with the scent…

"Thank you." Otis ducked his head, focusing on the dazed older wolf, murmuring soothing words and checking on the wound. He didn't move away until the EMTs arrived and Bree tugged at his shoulder to give them room.

"Boss?" Pedro mumbled as they loaded him on to a stretcher.

"I'm here." Otis gripped his hand. "I'm coming to the hospital. It's going to be okay."

Pedro mumbled something else, his words slurring together as his eyes drifted closed. Fury crackled through Otis' chest, filling him up until he could hardly speak.

He turned to Bree. "Go straight to Zacharias' apartment. Call me the second you get there."

"Okay."

For once, she didn't argue. Instead, she squeezed his hand and rocked up on her toes to kiss his cheek before she left.

He couldn't even enjoy the moment.

Whoever did this would pay.

Chapter 13

B ree may have been temporarily benched, but that didn't mean she was useless. The second the elevator doors to Zacharias' apartment closed behind her, she pulled out her phone and started calling the werewolves.

Otis probably told them already, but just in case, they should be warned. Someone out there was targeting the pack.

"Do you think it's the same person who attacked Silver Bullet? Who burned down your apartment?" Claire hovered at Bree's elbow as Micah hung up the line, promising to spread the word.

Bree glanced at her friend. Claire's red hair was wild and paint-splattered, and she wore her ancient painting overalls and no socks. In the far corner of the apartment, next to the pool, she'd set up a canvas and easel, with tins of paint scattered around an old sheet. Most days, Claire worked at the studio in her old bungalow, but Bree guessed she was on edge. Nervous about the attacks in the town.

Bree didn't blame her for wanting Zacharias close. Not one bit.

"Maybe." Bree frowned, gnawing at her thumbnail. "But there's no pattern. What do Charlton, the pack and I all have in common?"

"Well. You." Claire looked sorry to even say it. "Have you, um. Have you pissed anyone off lately?"

Bree snorted. It was such a Claire question. They'd been friends since middle school, and in all those years, Claire had displayed an incredible talent for very politely putting her foot in her mouth.

"I think we already know the answer to that," Zacharias called from the hammock slung by the bookshelves.

"Piss off, vamp," Bree yelled back before slinging an arm around her friend's shoulders. "Come on, Claire-Bear." She shifted her arm, wrinkling her nose at the wet paint smudged on her skin. "Let's solve a crime."

It was easier said than done.

Even after dragging Claire's easel over to the kitchen, propping up her giant sketchpad and writing the word 'suspects', they drew a blank. Bree hummed and started a new list, entitled 'motives'.

Nothing.

"Gods, this is impossible." She threw herself down in a chair and sagged over the kitchen table. "How does Danny do it?"

"By trying for more than thirty seconds?" Zacharias strolled up to the table, eyeing the two words scrawled on the easel. "Your handwriting is awful, by the way."

"Play nice." Claire smacked his leg. Zacharias plucked the pen off the table and turned to the sketchpad, his long-sleeved white shirt stretching over his shoulders.

"This is Boiling River," he said as he wrote on the pad, drawing out the letters in painstaking cursive. "Not a cute

91

fishing village. We've probably got at least three psychopaths running around at any one time. These don't need to be related. They don't even need a motive. It could be demons, or drunk tourists, or business competitors. Or, hell—it could be some poor asshole with sun stroke."

The vampire stepped back with a flourish. Bree and Claire leaned in together, both squinting at the looping words.

"And you think my handwriting's shit," Bree muttered under her breath. Zacharias shot her a glare.

Beneath the 'suspects' list, Zacharias had written two words: ex-lovers and lenders.

"You're in debt, correct?"

"Yes," Bree ground out. No point lying.

"And you have a long track record of casual flings."

"Zacharias," Claire hissed, shooting an apologetic look at Bree, but she leaned closer, pursing her lips.

She'd hooked up with guys, sure. Both humans and supernatural creatures. But rarely, and not since Claire and Zacharias started dating and Otis was everywhere she looked.

Why now? Why target her now?

"It's not an ex." She shook her head. "The timing doesn't make sense." She was ready to argue her point, but Zacharias nodded and crossed it off with a single black line.

Bree sat back in her chair and sighed.

"And I am in debt—thank you for that—but to the bank, not to the mob. I hardly think my bank manager is going to sabotage my finances."

Zacharias huffed and tossed the pen on the table.

"This is more fun in movies." He dragged out a seat, sitting down next to Claire. Though Bree loathed to agree with Zacharias on anything, he had a point. In the movies, there were incident rooms plastered with maps and red string. There were resources and neat, snappy answers.

When her phone buzzed against the table, she scooped it up with relief. Let it be good news. Let someone else have solved the problem.

"Bree?" Charlton's gravelly voice sounded in her ear. "Heard there were more attacks. You okay?"

It was typical Charlton. Clipped and gruff. He'd always been that way, even when she crashed on his sofa for two weeks last year while her apartment building was exorcised. He'd barely ground out full sentences to her, but he'd brought her clean blankets and a spare pillow. And every morning when she woke up, he fixed them both a fried breakfast and poured her coffee fresh from the pot.

"I'm good." A faint smile played on her lips, and she scratched at the table. She hadn't expected him to call. He wasn't really family, after all.

Even though he bought her birthday gifts every year. And taught her how to drive her motorbike at eighteen.

"Are you okay? How's the clean up going?" She'd offered to help, but Charlton had told her to get on and get another job. Said he was fixing the Silver Bullet up to sell; that he was too old for this shit.

She couldn't blame him. The bastard was older than he looked, and he looked pretty damn worn.

"Coming on." That was it. He was a man of few words. "Those wolves did a number on it, though."

"It wasn't them. They're being targeted too, C."

He grumbled something unintelligible, but the disbelief was clear in his tone.

"Be careful," was all he said, then the phone clicked and the line fell quiet. Bree sighed and dropped it to the table, looking up at two sets of worried eyes.

"Screw this," she announced, pushing her chair back. "There's only one answer. Cocktails."

* * *

For a vampire's fancy underground lair, the apartment was kind of creepy at night. Shortly after midnight, Zacharias and Claire made their excuses and retreated to the bedroom, sneaking love-struck glances at each other that made Bree want to barf.

She curled up on the sofa, swaddled in a fine knit throw, and cranked up the volume on the TV to block out the faint sound of giggling.

Gods-damned couples. Kill her now.

Except…

Bree had never been the sentimental type. She stamped out every last flicker of that in herself when her family moved away without her. Tying yourself to another person that way, making yourself so freaking vulnerable—the thought made her chest constrict like a vise.

But if she was honest with herself, really honest, and gods knew the cocktails helped with that… Bree was a teeny bit jealous. Somewhere deep inside her brain, she wanted that kind of bond.

To be missed. To watch someone's face light up when she walked in the room. To get antsy when they were apart for too long.

"Screw it." Bree dug out her phone from between the sofa cushions, dialing with one eye screwed shut. Otis picked up on the second ring, his voice warm and rich in her ear.

"Everything okay?"

"Yup." Bree flicked a piece of lint off her lap. "Why? Do I need to be in danger to call you?" Otis chuckled, and the knot in Bree's gut eased. If he was laughing, that meant Pedro was okay, and none of the other wolves were hurt.

"Micah said you called." In the background, Bree heard the echo of footprints and the ding of a bell. Across the apartment, the light above the elevator doors glowed on. Bree grinned and swung her legs off the sofa.

"Yeah." She wrapped the blanket around her shoulder, balancing the phone between her ear and shoulder as she walked. She'd spent so much damn time in this apartment over the last few days, she weaved between the dim shadows of furniture by memory.

The only lights were the blue-green glow of the pool, and an orange halo of lamplight by the far bookshelves. Bree stopped in front of the elevator doors, squeezing her arms around her waist.

It might not be him. It could be anyone—one of Zacharias' nocturnal buddies, or a neighbor, or Danny here with more bad news.

When the elevator doors swept open, Bree smiled. Of course it was him.

Otis looked exhausted, his t-shirt wrinkled and dark shadows clinging to his eyes. But he beamed when he saw her, his face shifting into well-worn creases, and something swelled in Bree's chest.

She could have what Claire and Zacharias had, if she wanted to.

All she had to do was reach out and take it.

"Everything okay?" She spoke in hushed tones, not ready to share Otis' presence with the others yet. He nodded, stepping out of the elevator and into her space. She tilted her head back.

"It is now."

His lips found hers, his arms winding around her body, and Bree clutched his shirt as she sighed into his mouth. The blanket slipped off her shoulders, forgotten, her phone dropping into the pile too, and Bree sucked in a breath as Otis scooped her into his arms.

Bree was not a small woman. She had substance, meat on her bones and height to her frame—a fact that she'd always rather liked. But she'd also made her peace long ago with the idea that no man would ever literally sweep her off her feet.

She hadn't accounted for Otis Pascale. Alpha werewolf, longtime enemy and secret dreamboat.

"You'll put your back out," she murmured against his lips. He carried her easily across the apartment, his amber eyes bright in the gloom.

Otis chuckled. "Have some faith, Mendez."

"It's not my strong suit."

"So I've noticed. But try anyway."

They smiled at each other, and Bree could feel the understanding forming between them. It was like a thread that tethered them, rib cage to rib cage, was growing stronger, tied with firmer knots.

"Claire and the vamp are in the bedroom," she warned. Otis changed direction, heading across the cavernous apartment.

He took her to the farthest corner, tucking them away behind a freestanding bookshelf. It was a reading nook—one that Zacharias had created once Bree started crashing with him and he 'wanted some gods-damned space'. In here, no prying eyes would find them. It was the closest they'd been to privacy since that night in Otis' bed.

"We'll have to be quiet," Bree murmured as he set her down on a polished desk. "Think you can handle that, wolf?"

Otis grinned, showing his sharp, white teeth.

"You know I love a challenge."

He seemed different in the shadows. Maybe it was the waxy moon hanging over the mountains tonight, or maybe it was the leftover adrenaline of Pedro's attack. Hell, maybe it was her.

But the jovial, teasing Otis was gone. This man was wild, all teeth and claws. He nipped at her jaw, and Bree wound her arms around his neck, shivering and tugging him closer. He stepped between her legs, pressing against her aching core, and Bree let out a whimper.

A *whimper.*

Though they'd never done this before, never mapped each other's bodies with greedy hands or nipped at each other's lips until they drew blood, every motion felt familiar, somehow. Like coming home.

Like Bree had done all this before in a dream, and was only just remembering now.

Otis flicked open the button on her jeans. She wiggled to make room for his delving fingers.

"Shit," she hissed as he slid inside her underwear, finding her bundle of nerves like a homing beacon. He rubbed her in smooth, teasing motions, so slow she growled and bit at his neck.

Otis' laugh was hushed. "You sure you're not part wolf?"

Bree licked over the skin. "Maybe I am. Where it counts."

Otis hummed, gathering her closer. He liked that, pressing

the hardness in his jeans against her and thrusting slightly as he worked her with his fingers. His mouth trailed along her jaw, nibbling her earlobe, before dipping down the side of her neck.

He lingered over her pulse point, his muscles so tense that vibrations shuddered off him in waves. Then, apparently with great effort, he tore his mouth away and kissed her shoulder instead. Bree clung to him, her head tipping back, and stifled a moan as he slid a finger inside her.

She clamped down, her muscles spasming as she fell apart in his arms, his grip the only thing keeping her from melting onto the floor.

Bree came back to herself with her forehead leaned against his chest. Otis stroked her back in smooth circles, his lips pressed against her hair.

"Fleurmahngh," Bree said.

"Thank you," Otis replied. She could hear the grin in his voice. Sucking in a deep breath, she tipped her head back, lunging up to kiss him.

"Your turn," she whispered, reaching for his belt, but across the room, the bedroom door slammed open.

"Otis?" Zacharias called. "You there, man?"

"There's no justice in this world," Otis said sadly. He buttoned her up quickly, straightening her clothes and tucking her hair behind one ear. "This is how all vampire-werewolf grudges begin."

Bree slid off the desk, holding his outstretched hand, and patted him on the shoulder as they stepped out of the reading nook.

"No." Zacharias pointed at them as they crossed to the sofa. "Tell me you didn't. Not my reading nook."

"Alright, we won't tell you." Bree smirked as the vampire groaned, stomping off to the kitchen for some blood. Claire dropped onto the sofa, patting the cushion next to her.

"I'll see you tomorrow." Claire's eyes widened as Otis kissed Bree's forehead. "Stay near Zacharias."

"Lucky me," a voice called from the kitchen.

Bree tamped down the pinch of hurt in her chest. Of course Otis wasn't staying; he was the alpha of the werewolf pack. The man had a million things to do. Endless responsibilities.

He had still come to see her first. So when she smiled at him, she meant it.

"See you tomorrow," Bree murmured, shy for the first time in her life. A sly smile spread across Claire's face.

She'd never live this down. She, Bree Mendez, allergic-to-relationships Bree Mendez, was acting like a love-struck schoolgirl. Bree chewed on the inside of her cheek as Otis left, watching the damn fine view of his ass walking away.

No. Turned out, she didn't care.

Chapter 14

O tis strode down the Boiling River high street, squinting into the bright morning sunshine. All around him, shops and cafes were opening up, and locals hurried to work on foot or rattled past in their trucks. Hungover tourists clustered together on benches and around cafe tables, their shoulders hunched and their expressions dazed.

Yeah. Everyone always thought they could handle Hex Mex's specialty drinks, mistaking the little umbrellas and dry ice for something benign.

Nope. When a bar named a drink a Zombie Killer, Otis figured you should take their word for it. Especially in a town like Boiling River, where there was no such thing as an empty threat.

The town square was deserted, dotted with only a scraggly flock of vultures and the stone statue of a giant. Something buzzed in his pocket, and Otis pulled out his phone, a grin spreading across his face as he saw the caller.

"You're obsessed with me, Mendez."

"Piss off, wolf." Bree's voice was warm in his ear. Otis swung down a side road, suppressing the urge to jump up and click his heels. She'd called him more in the last three days than she had in all the years she'd known him. "Just checking in. Where are you?"

Otis eyed the Supernatural Airwaves building across the street. It was a tumbledown wreck of a building, with a list of needed repairs a mile long, but they'd brightened it up with one of Claire's whacky murals. The pale brick front was splashed with bright purples and yellows and greens, and the shapes looked like different creatures depending on how you tilted your head.

"Work," Otis lied, carrying on down the street. "Just stepping inside the lobby now." The sidewalk echoed under his boots, like the paving stones were calling out to Bree that her would-be mate was a gods-damned liar. "You still with Zacharias?"

"Uh-huh," Bree said dryly. "We're becoming best friends." Down the line, a voice yelled something in the background.

At any other time, Otis would offer to come get her. To let her spend the day with him instead of the vamp. Not that Bree was some damsel in distress, but she was human, and though he loved Boiling River, it was still a town of bloodthirsty psychos.

It wasn't weak to be careful when some nut-job was targeting her. It was just good sense.

Today, though, Otis bit back the offer. He had no intention of going to the station today. And where he was headed—well, it was better all round if Bree never needed to know.

Otis rubbed the back of his neck as he walked. It didn't feel good, lying to her. It didn't sit right under his skin. His gut was tied up in knots, and he felt like he needed an hour-long scalding hot shower.

He was protecting her. He reminded himself of that fact, giving himself a small shake. This wasn't about how he felt; this was about the bastard who'd attacked his wolves and burned down Bree's apartment.

Otis had an idea, but he had to be sure.

Because if he was right, it would break Bree's heart.

* * *

The Boiling River police force was big considering the small size of the town. It made sense: you couldn't police rampaging supernaturals with a handful of pot-bellied old cops.

No; the Boiling River force counted dozens in its ranks. Men and women; human and supernatural. They were all crammed in here, in a one-time office building, ready to pile out at a moment's notice.

The station lay on the outskirts of town. Far enough away that people didn't feel watched, but close enough to get anywhere in a hurry. The force had taken over the building from an old paper company, and even years later, the air inside still smelled like warm envelopes and burned coffee. Electronics hummed constantly in the offices, behind blinds lowered over the glass windows to shut out prying eyes, and phones rang off the hook.

"Are you here about Pedro, Mr Pascale?"

A young troll constable sat behind the front desk, barely glancing at Otis as he typed. Of course he knew about Pedro; word traveled fast in Boiling River, and even faster around the precinct.

"No. I'm looking for Danny. The leopard shifter?"

He probably should have paid more attention to Officer Danny's rank. The troll's eyes flicked to him, then he leaned over and snatched up the phone.

"Sarge? Werewolf's here to see you. No, the alpha." The troll frowned, running his gaze over Otis more deliberately. "Seems fine to me."

Otis could just make out the crackle of Danny's reply, then the troll slammed the phone back in its cradle.

"Level Two. Room fourteen."

Otis took his sweet time as he wandered to the stairwell. He'd been here plenty of times before, picking up a rowdy werewolf pup or answering questions about scraps with the vampires. The precinct was almost friendly, it was so familiar, but as he strained to listen in on the murmurs around him, that warm feeling faded.

The cops whispered about the attacks.

Wondered who did it.

Wondered if he was involved.

Otis gritted his teeth, his mood soured, and pushed through the doorway into the stairwell.

He found Danny sat behind a cluttered desk, a towering pile of paper files in his in-tray. The day had barely begun, but already the shifter looked harangued, with tired eyes and an ink-smudge on his left cheekbone. If he was one of Otis' wolves, he'd have sent the man home and told him to get some gods-damned sleep.

"Morning," he said instead, pushing inside the office uninvited. "Have you found who's attacking my pack yet?"

"It's not just your pack." Danny rubbed his forehead, frowning down at an open newspaper. "The Silver Bullet bar and an apartment building were attacked too, remember."

"Yeah, about that." Otis dragged out the spare chair and dropped into it, the splayed metal legs groaning. "What are you thinking?"

Danny leveled him a look. "I think I can't discuss this with you."

"No?" Otis flicked at a pot of pens. "Not even if I can be useful?"

The sigh that gusted out of Danny seemed to travel up from the soles of his boots.

"If you have pertinent information, please pass it on. Otherwise—"

"I want you to check out Charlton Smith."

Danny paused. "The bar owner?"

"Exactly."

Danny waited for Otis to explain himself, the line deepening in his forehead. When Otis said nothing, he threw up his hands.

"His bar was destroyed! Why would—"

"You saw those claw marks. No werewolf made those."

Danny fell quiet, thinking. That first day at the bar, Bree had pointed it out: the height was all wrong for a werewolf. Otis glowed with pride at the memory.

"It's far-fetched…"

"It's just a theory," Otis agreed. "But I know it in my gut. Something's off with that guy. And twice now, I've caught a whiff of scent… it might not be him. But maybe it is."

"The two buildings both belong to him," Danny mused. "There could be a link, even if he didn't do it."

"There ya go." Otis slapped his thighs. "Now let's go do some digging."

Danny spluttered. "You can't investigate with me, Pascale. It's not Take Your Werewolf to Work Day."

Chapter 14

"You won't even know I'm there."

"Absolutely not."

"Thanks, man. I knew you'd come around."

Chapter 15

It was easy enough to give Zacharias the slip. He was a half-hearted bodyguard at best—sure, he didn't want anything bad to happen to Bree, but he was also fairly lukewarm about her company. Claire, on the other hand, had his undivided attention, and tended to wander around the apartment in tiny shorts, vest tops, and little else.

Also, Zacharias was a vampire. Even the most diligent of vampire bodyguards couldn't follow Bree outside in the daytime. She tried to feel bad as she hopped down his apartment building steps, tipping her face back to bask in the sunshine.

Nope. Bree was a grown-ass woman, and she could look after herself. There may be a bloodthirsty psycho running around Boiling River, but honestly, what else was new?

She had a stake in her backpack. A spray can of mace in her pocket. Bree was ready to rock. And the voice mail she'd received from her bank manager this morning was a timely reminder: life goes on.

Though she'd spent plenty of days cursing Boiling River in the past, especially after her family left, Bree had to admit the town was unlike anywhere else. It was kind of annoying—she'd scrimped and saved for months, paring down her budget so she could finally go on the backpacking trip of her dreams. She'd imagined all the wonders she'd see; the new cultures and sights and smells.

Then she got out of the valley, and realized within a few weeks: nowhere was weirder than Boiling River. There was a reason the tourists came here by the bus load, hanging out of the windows and snapping blurry photos of every street and local.

Any one of those tourists might kill to stay here. But it was a hard town to settle in, with its inhabitants verging on feral.

Most people had to be born to it. Like Bree. The idea didn't rankle her the way it used to.

Bree hid her smile, digging out her cell phone and calling the reason behind her change of heart. He'd always dragged her back here, the force of their bond undeniable, even to her. But now that she'd turned to him, accepted him…

It was so damn good to hear his voice. They chatted quickly, Bree biting her lip and smiling at the sidewalk like an idiot. Otis talked about coming into work, and Bree's feet changed direction of their own accord.

The job hunt could wait for half an hour. She just wanted to see him, feel his eyes on her skin. Maybe drag him into one of the radio station's broom closets.

The air was cool in the Supernatural Airwaves lobby. Bree squeezed through the front entrance, the door propped open with a brick, blinking as her eyes adjusted to the sudden gloom. The lobby was empty except for a battered vending machine, a community message board, and a figure slumped over in a chair.

"Olivia?"

Her friend peered up at her, her face in her hands and her elbows tucked into her waist. She looked awful—less healthy than half the ghosts that lived in the valley. Her cheeks were hollow, her lips pales and dry, and her eyes shone with tears behind her thick-framed glasses.

"Oh my gods." Bree hurried over, dropping to her knees in front of Olivia's chair. She patted over her friend's body, like there might be some wound she hadn't noticed. "What happened, Liv? What's going on?"

Olivia was already shaking her head. "Nothing."

"No," Bree growled, snatching Olivia's hand and squeezing. Her fingers were limp and cold. "Not nothing. Whatever has been going on with you, whatever secret you're keeping, it ends now." Bree leaned forward, forcing the other girl to meet her eyes. "Tell me, Liv. Tell me so I can help you."

Olivia sniffled, staring over Bree's shoulder at the worn carpet. Bree wanted to scream, wanted to take her by the shoulders and *shake*.

"Olivia. Please."

Her bottom lip wobbled. Olivia sucked in a shuddering breath, then let it out in a gust. Finally, she fixed her gaze on Bree, and her eyes were surprisingly clear.

"Do you hear that?" She jerked her head at the speakers clustered on the wall. The faint strains of the radio crackled through the wire mesh.

"The radio?"

"Yes. Anything else?"

Bree frowned, concentrating. A jingle was playing, with a

cheery ad script read over the top. Bree strained, trying to understand, but it was like Olivia had presented her with a puzzle with mostly missing pieces.

"It's a commercial," Bree said slowly. "For tarot readings in the emporium. Is that bad?"

Olivia slumped forward again, defeated. Bree rubbed her shoulder blades, trying to figure out what the hell she'd said wrong.

"I'm going mad," Olivia mumbled into her fingers. "It's happened. I've finally cracked."

"What are you—"

"Nothing." Olivia surged to her feet, putting Bree's nose level with the tortoiseshell button of her cable knit cardigan. "I just need to eat something. Or sleep." She rounded Bree, stepping over her legs, and marched toward the exit, her arms swinging with hands balled into fists.

"Liv!" Bree yelled after her, but Olivia waved over her shoulder without looking and stepped out into the street.

She could chase after her. Corner her friend and force her to admit what was wrong. Except Olivia was the most stubborn of all of them, and if she didn't want to talk, wild horses couldn't drag the words from her.

Bree was still kneeling, debating what to do, when Angie breezed into the lobby from the station corridor. The cupid brightened at the sight of Bree, her dark blunt bob swaying, but her face dropped almost immediately.

"Oh, Bree, I'm so sorry. Otis called in sick today. Is there anything I can help with?" Angie crossed to the vending machine, humming to herself before sliding in her quarters and selecting a bag of heart-shaped candies.

"I've got a sweet tooth." Angie smiled sheepishly over her

shoulder. As far as Bree could tell, everything about Angie was sweet. "It's a curse."

Finally remembering that she was kneeling on the ratty station carpet, Bree pushed to her feet.

"Otis called in sick?" The cupid's words were only just trickling through her brain, and with them, a cold, sickly feeling slid through her gut.

Just stepping inside the lobby now. That's what Otis had said. He'd told her he was in work; that he was walking inside.

Bree's heart thumped too hard in her chest. She swallowed around the lump in her throat.

Otis had lied.

* * *

Now more than ever, Bree wished she really was a wolf. Or a big cat shifter. Hell, even a vamp. Something vicious. Something that could *track*.

Because Bree wanted to find Otis Pascale and look him in the gods-damned eye as he told her the truth: Where he really was today. Why he'd lied to her.

And why he had to go and freaking ruin everything.

All these years, the same thing had held her back from accepting their bond. Bree didn't want *fated* anything. She was the captain of her own ship, the master of her own destiny, and she would not be told by some unknown force that Otis Pascale was the man for her.

She'd finally come around to it. Acknowledged that maybe that unknown force had good taste. Bree had made her peace with it, because at least this way, it was still her choice.

And now Otis had lied. He knew how important her

independence was to her; he knew this situation involved her too. And he'd taken her choices away anyway. Because how could Bree decide her own fate if she didn't have the information?

"Shit." Bree dug her phone out of her pocket. Doing this in person would be better, but she couldn't wait. "Freaking werewolves. Shit."

Her hands shook as she dialed. Her grip was clammy on the phone as she pressed it to her ear, pacing up and down the sidewalk outside Supernatural Airwaves.

"Hey." Otis answered right away, his voice warm and flirty. "Can't keep away, can you?"

Bree screwed her eyes shut, pinching the bridge of her nose. Then she forced a teasing lilt to her voice.

"Guess not. What are you up to, Pascale?"

"Just in my office." It came so easily to him.

"At the radio station?"

Otis snorted. "Where else?"

Right. Well, then. Bree dug the heel of her palm into her eye, grinding it roughly against the headache forming there. Until those words, she could have believed it was a mistake somehow. A misunderstanding.

But Otis lied twice, in those smooth, honeyed tones. What else had he lied about?

"That's interesting." The lightness dropped away from her voice. Bree let all the anger and bitterness bleed through her words. "Because I'm at the radio station right now."

"Bree…"

Wow. She could practically hear him sweating. She heard the exact moment he realized she'd caught him in a lie; that this fragile bond between them was severed.

"I can explain," he said urgently. "I'll come to you right now."

"No thanks," she said sweetly, and hung up. She squeezed her phone so hard the case cracked, digging the corner into her forehead. Something moved in the corner of her eye—it was Angie, waving at her from one of the Supernatural Airwaves offices.

Bree waved back, forcing a smile. It was her own damn fault. She knew nothing good would come of this.

You'd think she'd have learned when her family left her behind. Being vulnerable that way—putting her heart in the hands of another person—it was a fool's game.

Bree shoved her phone back into her pocket and set off down the street. It may be morning, but she needed a gods-damned drink.

Chapter 16

*S*hit.

    Shit, shit, shit.

    Shit on a gods-damned stick.

Otis paced up and down the sidewalk outside the precinct. He'd really done it this time. He'd put his stupid foot in his stupid mouth and wrecked any chance of something happening with Bree. He almost wished they'd never kissed; that they'd never had those stolen moments together in Zacharias' reading nook.

Now he knew what it felt like to hold her in his arms. To feel his fated mate holding him back. He knew the sound of her sighs; the taste of her lips.

Shit.

He'd never recover from this.

What was he thinking? He'd broken the fragile trust between them—the sacred trust between mates. He'd never have lied to her, not if he was thinking straight, but one poisonous thought had gnawed at his mind: how much it would hurt Bree if he was right.

Charlton was… something to her. Not quite a friend or family, but *something*. It would break her heart if Otis' theory was right—if it was the old bar owner he'd smelled near his cabin.

So he'd lied. Told her he was working in the radio station, so he could find out for sure before telling Bree his suspicions. And he'd sealed his fate in the process.

"Gods damn it." Otis kicked at a stone step. "You're an idiot, Pascale."

A siren rent the quiet morning air, screaming as a fire truck rounded the corner. It tore past, gusting the sidewalk with hot fumes, then rattled across the intersection and plunged towards the outskirts of town. Otis watched the fire truck go, his instincts nipping at his gut.

Something was wrong.

His phone began to buzz as he dug it out of his pocket. Micah's voice was strained in his ear, vibrating with suppressed aggression.

"Boss. Your cabin."

"Tell me."

Otis stared after the path of the firetruck, the siren wailing in the distance. Two cop cars pulled out of the precinct lot, tearing after the larger vehicle. He had a feeling he already knew.

"It's on fire."

Otis' spare hand balled into a fist, squeezing tight until his knuckles cracked. His cabin. His home. He'd built it with his own two hands; modeled it after the memories of those hiking trips with his father. His possessions were there, but more importantly, those rooms were filled with the ghosts of perfect moments.

Lazing with the pack in front of the fire. Late night barbecues with Angie and Zacharias. *Bree.*

"Gather the pack," Otis ground out, unable to keep the roughness from his voice. "Make sure everyone is accounted for, then go to Pedro's hospital room. Wait for me there."

"But your cabin—"

"It doesn't matter," Otis thundered. Gods. He never yelled, but today was testing even his gentle temper. He forced a more even keel into his voice. "It's just a building. It's a trap or a distraction; either way, we're not falling for it. Now gather the pack and get to the hospital."

"Yes, sir."

There was a subdued tone to Micah's voice—the hint of reproach.

Whatever. If he was pissed at Otis, he'd have to get in line. What the wolves didn't seem to understand, what Bree didn't get, was that he'd do anything to protect them.

He'd lie. Cheat. Steal.

Let his beloved cabin burn.

There were very few things he wouldn't do.

So when Otis took off jogging toward the radio station, he went with a clenched jaw and steel in his spine. Bree might hate him right now, but she was in danger.

He'd protect her, whether she liked it or not.

* * *

It took him longer than he liked to pick up Bree's scent. Boiling River was usually empty in the mornings, the whole town exhausted from a night of drinking and fighting. But apparently, everyone and their mom were out in the streets this morning. Scent trails criss-crossed over the sidewalks; a gnome on a coffee bike left burning scent lines of whole roast through the town square. Tourists huddled like flocks of geese, scuttling between shop fronts, and the locals' trucks belched fumes as they rattled down the streets.

Cafes threw their glass doors open, washing the sidewalks with the smell of fresh bread. The florist had set out a brand new display of fresh cut flowers; a shoe shine buffed a demon's boots with stinking polish.

Otis jogged through the Boiling River streets, barely resisting the urge to shove the florist's table over. Why today? Why did the town whip out their new scents in one wretched assault?

Bree had been at the station, all right. He'd found her trail out there on the sidewalk, practically pulsing with the sharp tang of her anger. And he'd followed where she'd turned on her heel, storming back the way she came. But Bree was not an easy woman to track.

The thing about hunting animals was that they were predictable. They made sense. An animal had a finite number of concerns and behaviors. Food. Water. Shelter. You could track an animal and its trail told a clear story.

Bree, on the other hand, was inexplicable. She'd charged away from Supernatural Airwaves and made a beeline towards the town square. Then she'd veered off to the side, pausing to pick up what smelled like a bag of warm, sugared doughnuts. Otis trotted in her footsteps, inhaling deeply, ignoring the growl of his stomach.

Bree had eaten the doughnuts, their scent quickly fading as she apparently swallowed them each in one gulp. Then she'd stopped for a few minutes on the edge of the town square, her trail colliding with the coffee bike gnome's.

Apparently Bree liked to eat her feelings. Otis filed that away for future reference. Maybe one day, far in the future, when the sting of his lie had faded away, he could win her back by the taco truck. Or he could cook her his dad's spaghetti carbonara.

After stopping to buy coffee, Bree's trail became… confused. She wandered to a bench. Went and sat by the fountain. Had some kind of altercation with a vulture. Otis wandered around the town square, sniffing deeply, ignoring the whispers of the nearby tourists at their cafe tables.

He probably looked mad. Well, he was about to look madder.

Otis ducked inside the tattoo parlor, nodding to the gargoyle hunched behind the glass counter.

"Hey, Gregor."

A pair of pale gray eyes flicked up and away.

"Hello."

"Do me a favor and watch my stuff?" Otis stripped as he talked, pulling his t-shirt over his head and reaching for his belt buckle. Gregor rolled his eyes, supremely unruffled.

"Leave them behind the counter. But I won't watch them."

"Thanks, man."

The gargoyle gusted out a sigh. He moved stiffly, his stone limbs grating together, but the sketch in front of him was ornate. Delicate.

"Nice," Otis said, stashing his clothes beneath the counter. Gregor sucked on his teeth and said nothing. "I'll be back soon."

Gregor raised a hand without looking, and Otis turned to face the doorway. His eyelids fell shut, and his stomach lurched as his body stretched and changed. Fur burst through the pores of his skin; his bones cracked and lengthened.

When Otis opened his eyes again, the colors of the street

outside were dulled. But the smells—they shouted at him, rioting in the still morning air.

Otis huffed in a deep breath and took off at a trot, finding Bree's scent immediately. In this form, he could taste her anger at him. The sour tang of her disappointment and secret hurt.

He'd make it up to her. Hell, he'd tell her everything from now on—more than she'd ever care to know. But first, he had to make sure she was safe.

Safe, and far from Charlton Smith.

Chapter 17

B ree knelt up on her stool, leaning across the scratched wooden bar. She'd come here on a whim, suddenly gripped with nostalgia as she moped around the town square.

This bar had been her life. The only constant of her days, shaping her routines for the last few years. She'd worked more shifts here than she could count; she'd invented new cocktails and dominated at pool. On a few messier nights, she'd danced on the bar, and when her head was clearer, she'd run a poker ring in the back room.

The Silver Bullet. Bree sighed. It was the closest thing she had to a home. And look at it now—its windows smashed and boarded, its furniture splintered and piled in a heap. Bree rocked on the stool she'd pulled from the tangle of wooden limbs, getting a wobble and warning creak in reply.

Bree twisted the cap off a whisky bottle and poured herself a finger's worth in a glass.

The old Bree would have skipped the tumbler altogether and

swigged straight from the bottle. She'd already be marching into the library to bother Olivia, or swaggering into Claire's cottage to rant.

Otis had changed her. Made her grow, even against her will. Bree huffed, pushing the drink away on the bar. She didn't really want it. She glanced around the bar instead, moisture welling up in her eyes.

He lied to her. She couldn't believe it.

Oh, she knew men lied. Women and creatures, too. But Otis had seemed so different. A tease, yes, a wind-up merchant—but he was so damn responsible when you really looked at him.

The career. The pack. The cabin he'd built with his bare hands. And his insistence that they were mates, that he was already committed to her, heart and soul...

Maybe more doughnuts would help. Bree slid off her stool just as a shape appeared in the doorway, blocking out the light from the street. Bree squinted, her shoulders tense, then relaxed when she recognized the shape of her old boss.

"Hey, Charlton."

The old codger shuffled inside, the metal chains from his bike leathers tinkling. He paused and shoved the door shut behind him, shutting them away in the gloom. Only two windows were unboarded, their pale shafts of light the only thing keeping the bar from full darkness.

"Bad day?" Bree asked as Charlton crossed the bar floor, his shoulders hunched and his mouth pinched in a scowl. He shook his head in a jerk, then grabbed another stool and carried it over to the bar. A pained sigh escaped his lips as he set it down beside her, heaving himself up to sit.

"Not a young man anymore," Charlton muttered, as if Bree might have thought otherwise. Even so, he moved stiffer than usual today. He must have overdone it again.

"I told you I'd help with the bar." Bree nudged him, then slid over her untouched drink. Charlton leveled her a look, but tossed it back all the same, hissing as he slammed the empty glass down on the wood.

"You've done enough," he muttered darkly. "Been quite the spokeswoman for the wolves."

Bree bristled. "They didn't do it. That's all. Don't you want to catch whoever really did wreck the bar? Whoever burned down my apartment?"

Charlton grumbled something under his breath, shifting on his stool. Now her eyes were growing used to the gloom, she saw the dark shadows under Charlton's bloodshot eyes. The overgrown scruff on his cheeks. Her old boss was a wreck, probably had been for days, and all the while she'd been flitting about, hooking up with Otis Pascale.

No wonder Charlton was so bitter. He'd been here for her so many times before; he deserved better from her now. Bree reached out and gripped his old, gnarled hand, rubbing her thumb over his knuckles.

"We'll fix the bar back up. To reopen or sell, whatever you want. I bet the wolves would help, you know, if we asked—"

"I won't have them here," Charlton spat. "Filthy animals."

Bree paused. Slowly, she withdrew her hand. She'd never heard Charlton talk like that before.

A grudge was one thing, unfounded suspicions another, but *hatred*?

"They're people too." Bree spoke quietly, forcing her voice steady. "Some of them are assholes, yes, just like people, but they're not animals—"

"They're the definition of animals." Charlton spoke louder,

faster, his knuckles whitening as he gripped the edge of the bar. "Snarling, wretched, uncontrollable beasts, prowling the town like it's their goddamn territory." A fleck of spittle flew onto the bar, stark against the dark wood. Bree watched it, dazed. "We'd be better without them, and the rest of the freaks here. Vampires and gnomes and gods-damned shifters…"

Charlton trailed off, muttering under his breath. He snatched for the whiskey bottle, pouring himself another slosh of liquid, and Bree wiped her palms down the front of her ripped jeans.

She swallowed. Cleared her throat. Gods, why was her mouth so dry? There were drinks here, things like water and juice too, but suddenly more than anything, she wanted to step back into the sunshine. She slid gingerly off her stool, her mind racing, and patted Charlton awkwardly on the shoulder.

"Better get back to it," she said, falsely bright, the floorboards creaking as she turned toward the door. A hand whipped out, fast as a rattlesnake, and gripped her elbow hard.

"Not so fast." Charlton's warm breath tickled her cheek, muggy with alcohol. Bree tugged at her arm, but his grip tightened, and her pulse thundered in her ears as he slid off his stool.

His boots landed heavily on the floorboards, and Charlton staggered to one side. Bree tore at his hold, but he was stronger than he looked, well-muscled under those ancient black leathers. He spun her round in one quick movement, pressing something cold and hard into the small of her back.

"Stay there," Charlton called, and it took Bree a few moments to realize he wasn't talking to her. A pair of amber eyes watched them from the shadows, creeping closer in the gloom.

Otis. Relief swept through her, chased quickly by a fresh bite of fear.

"Get out of here," she called, her voice wobbly but loud. "It's fine. Charlton won't hurt me." She tried to sound more confident than she felt, as if she could convince the unhinged old man gripping her elbow that way. The gun dug harder into her spine.

"You don't know what I'd do, girl." His breath was hot on her ear, his chest rising and falling against her arm. This wasn't the man who'd given Bree her first job; who'd bought her Christmas and birthday gifts; who'd let her crash on his sofa more than a few times.

This man was crazed. Sent out of his mind. Bree's heart cracked open for Charlton, for the gruff, kind old man she'd known, even as a wave of hatred swept through her chest.

He'd burned down her apartment. Attacked sweet, kind Pedro. Waged a war on these wolves, and for no freaking reason.

"Why?" Bree tossed over her shoulder as Charlton marched her forward. She felt rather than saw his shrug.

"Someone had to do something. Call it pest control."

She'd never call it that. But she kept him talking, because while Charlton huffed and ranted, those amber eyes crept closer and closer, burning bright in the dark.

It was hypnotic. Like standing in an ancient jungle, watching a beast stalk toward you, and being too spellbound by its beauty to run. Charlton's crazed rambling faded away, blurring into the background, and Bree heard only the thump of her heartbeat and the drag of breath into her lungs. Her awareness narrowed down to two things: the dig of cold steel into her back, and the rush of blood through her veins.

A floorboard creaked beneath Otis' paw. Charlton trailed off, suddenly remembering where he was. And Bree threw her body to the side, tearing from his grasp, as a gunshot rang out and glass shattered.

Bree landed on the floorboards, the breath knocked from her body. She rolled onto her side, head jerking up.

The wolf leaped.

* * *

The Boiling River werewolves were rowdy sometimes. The pups especially were pains in the ass, constantly knocking over trash cans or wrecking vegetable patches. Bree had often rolled her eyes at the enormous furry wolves capering past the bar windows, but she hadn't realized until this moment just how tame those pups were.

Otis was vicious. He was rage unleashed; a creature of the moon finally letting loose his powers. He moved with lithe grace, all bunching muscles and tendons as thick as Bree's arm, and she gaped as the huge black wolf tackled Charlton Smith to the floor.

Otis snapped and snarled, his fangs slicing through the air, but he didn't go for the throat, at least. Even now, in his most primal form, he restrained the worst of his instincts. Instead, he pressed the older man into the floorboards, smothering him with his bulk, and gave a rumbling growl each time Charlton tried to struggle.

It was over before it began. Of course it was—there was no contest here. Otis was a werewolf, the alpha of the pack, and more than that—he was in his prime. Even man against man, Charlton had no hope with his creaky joints and bleary eyes. He bellowed as Otis crushed him into the ground, thrashing and writing beneath the black, furry limbs. Bree pushed herself to her feet, her ears ringing from the stray gunshot, and stepped forward in a daze.

The wolf's great head swung around to stare at her, its amber eyes glowing bright in the darkness. And Bree watched, throat tight, as those eyes winced in pain, pupils constricting as another gunshot rang out.

Charlton shoved the werewolf onto the ground, staggering to his feet. He stood with his stocky legs planted apart, breathing hard, the gun gripped in his hand.

Charlton took aim, the barrel pointed between Otis' eyes. He flexed his fingers, adjusting his grip. Then he let out a grunt, dropping the gun with a clatter as he fell to the floor.

Bree stood behind the slumped body of her boss, a pool cue clutched in her hands. She stared at the blood seeping between his scruffy, silver hair, then up at the amber eyes watching her, still narrowed in pain.

Bree dropped the cue. She staggered back, hands raised.

Then she rushed to the bar phone.

* * *

"It's not funny." Otis winced as the EMTs crowded around him from behind, prodding at his wound. He straddled one of the bar chairs, still naked except for the dish cloth tossed over his lap, his eyes glued to Bree as she stood beside Danny.

"It is a bit funny," Bree heard Micah say, the coyote shifter lingering protectively at his alpha's side. His was the second number she'd called, after 911. "Think how heroic this could have been if you didn't get shot in the ass."

Bree shook her head, smiling down at the toes of her boots. Danny nudged her, pointing across the room.

On the other side of the bar, as far away as the EMTs could safely move him, Charlton was being patched up. His head wound had been checked and dressed, and a ridiculous white bandage was wrapped around his skull. Tufts of silvery hair sprouted between the strips of cloth, and Micah was right. It was almost funny.

Almost, but not quite. Not when Bree let reality sink in. Not as she watched the closest thing she had to family in Boiling River stumble through the door in handcuffs.

"That's one mystery solved." Danny didn't exactly sound pleased. Bree wondered what the hell else the leopard shifter had on his plate. It was hard enough to be a police officer in a normal town, but in Boiling River...

Well, there was no shortage of chaos.

"What happens next?" she asked. Her voice was hoarse. Bree wrapped her arms around her waist to stop the shivering. Danny shrugged, still frowning at the doorway where Charlton had left.

"He'll be charged. Kept away from here. And you go back to your life."

What life? Bree wanted to ask. Over the last few weeks, she'd lost everything. Her job, her pseudo-family, her home, her belongings. These days, her full-time job was being a pain in Zacharias' ass.

She didn't say those things out loud. They were her problems, no one else's, and she suddenly had a fierce desire to solve them all on her own. No special favors from Otis; no help from her friends. Just hard work and some kind of purpose.

An idea tickled in the back of her head.

"What about the bar?" she asked, sounding almost casual.

"It's up for sale." Danny scuffed his boot over the fine layer of dust and glass. "Some poor fool will take it on."

Some poor fool was right. Bree chewed her lip, a plan forming as she watched Otis limp out to the ambulance. He looked at her as he passed, his gaze intense, and she nodded but didn't smile.

She was poor. And a fool. She checked all the boxes.

Time to make one more call.

Chapter 18

⚜

He found her on the outskirts of town. Sitting on a boulder, with her legs drawn up and her chin resting on her knees, Bree looked like a dream. An embodiment of the sunset washing gold over the mountains ahead of her. Bree's warm skin and chocolate brown waves, glinting with strands of copper, reminded Otis of the heat which rolled off his cabin's wood burner in the evenings.

Before a mad old bastard burned his house down, anyway.

Still, Otis couldn't help the light feeling in his chest as he hopped up on the boulder beside her. His home may be lost—hers too, he reminded himself—but they were just buildings filled with *stuff*. Things.

Everything important was safe and well. His mate. His pack. His friends at the radio station. And now Otis got to watch the sunset beside the love of his life, his eyes widening in awe as the desert lit up in metallic hues.

Bree sighed. She didn't turn to look at him, but her mouth pressed into a tighter line.

"I'm surprised you can even sit down, Pascale."

He chuckled. "Wolves heal fast."

Bree grunted, then silence stretched between them. The grin slid off Otis' face.

This boulder was popular with local photographers. You could sit here and see the desert unfurled in front of you, stretching and undulating for miles like a dusty, wrinkled picnic blanket. Cacti lurched out of the baked dirt, holding up their arms in surrender, and boulders were scattered haphazardly like giant dropped crumbs.

There were fissures in the earth: jagged wounds which swallowed the rays of light and tourists alike. Columns of steam billowed toward the sky from some of them, the heated water below building up then exploding with a shriek. Sometimes spirits moaned out too, riding the steam currents out of the depths below.

Snakes slithered. Scorpions sparred, their barbed tails held high. And yet somehow, in this merciless landscape, the dominant feeling was one of calm.

"You lied to me." Bree didn't sound angry. It was worse—she was resigned.

"I did." Otis licked his lips, heart clenching. He wouldn't try to hide from what he'd done. But perhaps if she could understand... "I suspected Charlton might have been involved. I caught a whiff of his scent near my cabin. But I didn't want to tell you until I was sure. I didn't want to hurt you, Bree."

She hummed, nodding her head slightly. Her chin stayed glued to her knees, patches of her golden skin peeking through her ripped jeans. Gods, he wanted her.

"That makes sense."

She didn't sound any happier. Otis stared out at the valley, gut churning.

"I'll never do it again. I swear, Bree. It was a stupid mistake, but I know better now."

Her sigh shivered down his spine. That was not the sound of a willing mate. The sound of a person who was about to deliver good news. And when Bree finally looked at him, exhaustion and sorrow swimming in her eyes, she didn't even need to say the words.

Otis clenched his jaw and nodded. He wouldn't push her. He'd respect his mate's decision.

Even if that meant spending the rest of his days alone. Yearning for her, pining like a pup, kicking himself over a stupid, pointless lie.

Otis turned his head to stare at the desert, blinking away the moisture brimming in his eyes. And Bree tipped her head over, leaning against his shoulder with a tiny huffed breath.

This hurt her too. But it was what she wanted. Otis let his eyes fall shut, feeling the warmth of her against his side. Flyaway strands of her hair tickled his cheek, but he didn't brush them away.

He didn't move until long after she left, sliding down off the boulder and walking slowly back to town. He sat there and watched the desert valley; listened to the creatures moving in the shadows and the gentle chorus of crickets. When a wolf's howl rent the night air, the ghost of a smile flitted over his face.

"Come on, then," Otis muttered to himself, sliding off the boulder and rubbing the bullet wound on his ass. "Get your shit together, Pascale."

* * *

Chapter 18

The wolves lived scattered throughout Boiling River, some in cramped bed sits and others in lush townhouses. Anyone might mutate in their teenage years and become a werewolf, regardless of race, riches or creed. Jason lived with his parents in an apartment building with a full-size salt water pool; others in the pack lived in mobile homes and adobe cottages out in the desert.

Any of them would have housed Otis without question. He was their alpha, but more than that, he'd offered them all shelter plenty of times. All it would take was a single text, and he'd have access to a spare bed and hot shower.

Otis rolled over beneath his desk, wincing at the stains on the carpet. He didn't want to know. If he'd learned anything since buying up this building for the radio station, it was that sometimes, ignorance was bliss.

The speakers in the corner of his room rattled out a faint stream of music. He'd cranked the volume down as low as it would go, but the speakers would not switch off. He'd tried unplugging them, cutting them off from all power; he'd taken the casing apart with a screwdriver. Still, the music hummed through the speakers, nestling innocently on his wall.

Fine. They could stay on. Some noise was probably good for him, anyway. Otherwise he'd be left with nothing but the scratch of the carpet and his own thoughts, circling round and round his head.

"Oh, good." Zacharias kicked the door open, swaggering inside. The vampire looked as he always did: carelessly stylish, pristinely rested, and less than thrilled to find himself there. "I bet Angie twenty bucks you were being tragic somewhere. Drinks tonight are on her."

Otis gestured up the length of the musty blanket covering

131

his body.

"I'm sleeping, not drinking. And there are no bars left, anyway."

"There's always Hex Mex," Zacharias mused.

"We're not that desperate."

Zacharias snorted and dropped into Otis' desk chair.

"Speak for yourself. You're not the one with Bree Mendez living on your sofa."

"Don't rub it in, vamp."

"And besides," Zacharias continued, ignoring him completely. "You've dragged me to Hex Mex plenty of times."

"Because you're an antisocial bastard who needs to be socialized. Like a traumatized dog."

Zacharias clapped and launched to his feet. "A compromise, then. To keep my antisocial tendencies from creeping back in."

Angie poked her head around the door frame as if summoned. Her face scrunched up when she saw Otis curled up in the shadows beneath his desk.

"Oh, Otis. Don't lie down there. We never clean."

Zacharias stuck his hand out, fingers wiggling. "Pay up, cupid. If we're having a tragic sleepover in here, we're going to need booze. And blood."

"Aren't you disgustingly rich?" Angie asked lightly, slapping a bill into his palm.

"Every little helps." Zacharias winked and disappeared through the doorway. Otis watched, propped up on one elbow, as Angie picked her way gingerly through the mess in his office. He always meant to get around to sorting through these boxes, but somehow, he started every day with a To Do list three miles long.

"I'm not being tragic," he told her. "I'm sleeping."

Angie climbed into his chair, grabbing the desk as it began to spin. She tucked her short legs beneath her body, her many baggy sweaters pooling around her and hiding her limbs. When Angie cocked her head at him, her black bob quivered.

"Are you certain?"

Otis thought for a moment. "I'm eighty percent sure."

Angie smiled, settling back in his chair, gazing around at the mishmash of photos and posters hung on his office walls. This was how Otis liked to remind himself he wasn't lonely: with constant visual reminders of all his loved ones on every surface.

There were no photos of Bree. They hadn't spent enough time together to take one, and it would be creepy to get hold of one without her knowing.

No. Otis had to mentally add pictures of his mate to his walls. Her wild, brown waves; her soft curves. That fiery spark in her eyes.

Angie cleared her throat softly. Otis jerked and smiled at her sheepishly.

"There's nothing to be ashamed of." Angie plucked at a loose thread on her sleeve. "Love is a gift. It's good to be grateful."

The cupid could read your heartbreak on your face as easily as a road sign. Otis collapsed back against the carpet, letting his head rest on the mystery stains.

"I had one shot. One mate. And I blew it, Ange."

She clicked her tongue. "We'll see."

Zacharias burst back through the doorway before he could respond, brandishing a bottle of whiskey in one hand and a bottle of blood in another.

"Enough of your cupid propaganda," he declared, slamming the bottles down on the desk. The wood quaked above Otis, showering him in sawdust and spiders. "We deal with this like men."

"Oh, good," Angie said dryly, even as she reached for the whiskey. "That sounds much healthier."

Otis lay stretched out on the carpet, listening to them bicker, and let his eyes fall shut for a moment. He could kick them out. Assert some of his commanding alpha energy and finally get some peace. But his chest ached at the thought, and Otis sighed and tossed his musty, ancient blanket to one side.

"Make room." His shoulder knocked Angie's chair as he crawled out. "Heartbroken wretch coming through."

"That's the spirit." Zacharias produced a glass from somewhere and poured Otis a generous measure. Then he thrust the drink down to where Otis still knelt, tearing the stopper out of the blood bottle with his teeth.

"To an absolute train wreck of a day," the vampire said, raising his bottle. Angie clinked it with her glass, then reached toward Otis.

He huffed a laugh. Shook his head, and knocked his glass against both of their drinks.

"Cheers," he said, and tipped the drink back, feeling the burn of whiskey at the back of his throat.

An absolute train wreck of a day.

Yeah. That about covered it.

Chapter 19

T HREE MONTHS LATER.

Bree woke before the sunrise—never a good sign. She was a creature of the night, through and through, and whenever her brain nudged her out of bed before ten, she couldn't help but feel betrayed.

Rain pounded on her bedroom window, beating against the glass panes. Rain in the desert. Another omen, although she begrudgingly allowed that it was perhaps not a bad one. It rained in Boiling River maybe twice a year, if they were lucky, and a good drenching was usually cause for celebration. The desert creatures pierced the air with their cries, and the tired plants in the locals' gardens sighed and unfurled their leaves.

Bree lay for a moment, listening to the drumming raindrops and counting her slow breaths. Her attic bedroom was cramped—so cramped that she could practically reach up an arm and graze the low ceiling with her fingertips. Regardless, she still woke each morning dazed with her good luck.

Her own place. A home. One that wouldn't be snatched out from under her because of a missed rent payment; one that she could redecorate and paint the walls. She'd painted her bedroom walls bright white, with an accent wall in amber.

She'd rather not think about why.

Giving up on any hopes of more sleep, Bree growled and tossed her covers back. She stooped as she moved around the room, rummaging in her drawers for a paint-splattered t-shirt and torn jeans. Today was no day for her best clothes. Not until tonight, at least. Today would be a long day of manic, last-minute preparations.

A scalding hot shower eased her aching muscles, still stiff from yesterday's work. It was probably a good thing, Bree mused, that she had no idea how much hard work this place would be when she put in her offer. She might have balked and gone back to her old ways of crappy jobs and crappier apartments.

No. Bree smiled at nothing as she soaped her shoulder, rolling her neck and hissing with relief. She wouldn't change the last few months for the world.

A tiny voice whispered in the back of her head that there was one thing she might change. One decision she'd made while dazed and heartbroken, too overwhelmed to really think straight. Doing this place back up, rebuilding with her bare hands, rebuilding her life... she couldn't help but wonder what it might have been like if *he* had been here...

Bree huffed, pushing the thoughts from her mind. No point dwelling on the past. That kind of thinking was what screwed her over the first time around, leaving her purposeless and lonely, pining after a family that was long gone.

She didn't do that shit anymore. Bree was looking to the

future.

The sky was still dark outside the windows as Bree clomped down the stairs in her work boots twenty minutes later. Dust dulled the glass, and she made yet another mental note to run around with a duster before tonight. So many tasks and tiny worries—every time she solved one issue, three more popped up in its place. It was as maddening as it was thrilling, her hours rocketing forward as she clung on by her fingernails.

Bree set the coffee to brew, chewing on her thumb knuckle as she peered out of the cramped kitchen window. The Silver Bullet was never intended as a home. It barely had working bathrooms when she bought it. The last three months had been about two goals: rebuilding the bar to open it again, and fixing it so she could live here too. Sure, she knew full well that living above a bar would be a pain in the ass sometimes. Rowdy customers; nosy drunks; only stolen moments to herself.

Bree didn't care. This was it for her. She knew it as soon as the idea crossed her mind all those months ago. And to her eternal surprise, Zacharias had known it too, agreeing to loan her the money with barely any convincing.

"If it gets you off my sofa and out of my apartment, Bree Mendez, I will gift you the money. No payback required."

"Shut up," she'd said, choking down a laugh. Disbelief and joy warred inside her. *"I don't want favors. I'll pay you back with interest, vamp."*

"See that you do," he'd intoned, faux threat in his voice. Apparently he didn't hate her as much as he claimed. And now he was the guest of honor to tonight's opening, with a row of premium blood bottles lining the bar fridge.

The scent of fresh coffee wafted up as Bree poured a mug, slurping greedily at the scalding liquid. She hissed, burning her tongue, but went back for more anyway, then finally added a slosh of milk. The china warmed her palms, and she leaned against the counter, inhaling deeply through her nose.

This was it. The big night. The reopening of the Silver Bullet; the first night of the rest of her life. She'd plastered the town with invitations; she'd called round the tour operators and offered special deals.

There would be crowds. She was sure of it. And maybe even *him.*

He'd kept his distance the last few months. Respected her decision almost an annoying amount. Whenever Bree passed Otis Pascale in the Boiling River streets, he smiled at her and kept walking. She'd been grateful at first, in desperate need of the space, but as time wore on it stung.

Every time she'd see him, striding toward her with those broad shoulders and that wide, easy smile. Her heart would swell in her chest, every atom of her body screaming at her to reach out and touch his skin. Then Otis would pass, not even slowing his stride, and her rib cage cracked open and bled.

She'd written his invitation by hand, her throat tight as she scratched out the letters. What if he'd moved on? What if she'd severed their tie somehow, and he didn't want her anymore?

There was only one way to find out. Maybe tonight wasn't the best night to try, but Bree didn't do things in half measures. She could open her bar and declare her love in one night—no big deal.

Bree shook her head and snatched for the coffee pot again.

* * *

Drums shivered in the background as the band tuned up on

their platform. Bree had gone all out for tonight, booking up the local demon band and putting in a state of the art sound system. Spotlights hung from the ceiling, pointed at the small stage, and the band posed moodily as they checked their levels.

Twenty minutes. The Silver Bullet doors would open in twenty minutes, and the crowd she could already see gathering on the sidewalk outside would flood through her doors. Bree rubbed her palms down the front of her black pants, trying her best to ignore the tremble in her fingertips.

She wasn't nervous. Bree Mendez did not get nervous. She was a badass—at least she tried to tell herself so. She'd worked so freaking hard for this, and she knew better than anyone in Boiling River what made an incredible night out.

It was happening. It was real.

And he was coming.

Otis had texted her mid-morning, her phone buzzing as she balanced on top of a stepladder, focusing the spotlights. She'd tugged it out of her back pocket, the step ladder wobbling, and stared at his message with her nose two inches from the screen.

Otis: I wouldn't miss it. :)

A smiley face? What the hell did that mean? Was that a so-glad-we're-friends-now smiley face, or a I've-missed-you-too-let's-have-babies face?

Bree stuffed her phone back into her pocket, mind racing. Gods, she sucked at this love thing.

The bar tonight was barely recognizable compared to its previous shabby shell. Oh, the furniture was still old and worn—no point wasting money given the beating bar furniture got—but she'd spruced it up with a lick of dark paint, and sanded and re-varnished the floorboards too.

The windows sparkled. The spotlights dazzled, while patches of suggestive darkness still gathered in the corners of the room. Bree wanted a seductive vibe. A wild vibe. A bar where people came to feel glamorous and exciting.

"Looks good," the lead singer of the band called over. He tossed his bleached hair out of his eyes and winked. Bree nodded, shooting him a polite smile before retreating behind the bar to double-check the stock levels one last time.

Freaking demons. Some things never changed.

When the clock struck 7pm, the troll bouncer she'd hired tugged the doors open. The crowds poured inside, crashing like a wave through her perfect bar, chattering loudly as they gaped at the changes. Some clustered around the new pool tables and dart boards; others tried their luck with the smirking band members. Most headed straight for the bar, hard excitement glinting in their eyes.

"You've got this," Bree told the team of three bartenders she'd hired. A human girl, freshly graduated from high school; a young gargoyle she'd found hunkered on the bar roof; and Jason, one of the werewolf pups. Jason shot her a cocky grin.

"I think we can handle a bunch of tourists," he said, then was promptly inundated with calls for whisky and beer. Bree smirked, pulling a bottle of premium blood out of the refrigerator, and passing it to Zacharias where he lounged at the end of the bar.

"Not bad." Zacharias hid a smile as he surveyed the room, bustling with life. "You can pay me back sooner than I'd thought."

"Shut up." Bree punched his shoulder, grinning, as Claire arrived too, looping her arms around the vampire's waist. He bent his head, breathing deeply from her hair, then kissed her before swigging from his bottle. His fangs glinted as he lowered his drink, and he flicked one with his tongue as he watched the crowd. The drums shivered again, then grew louder, and screams echoed as the band launched into their set.

"It's a nice touch." The voice came from behind her: deep and smooth and warm. Bree spun around, ignoring Zacharias' snort behind her. Otis leaned on the bar, chiselled and gorgeous in a midnight blue button-down shirt with the sleeves rolled to his elbows. His forearms were corded with muscle and tendons, his dark hands flecked with old scars.

"What?" Bree asked stupidly. He was here. He really came.

"The band." Otis' mouth quirked up on one side. "The gods know we need more excitement in Boiling River."

It was a joke, clearly, but Bree's laugh came out strangled and weird. Jason shot her a worried look as he pulled a pint beside her, but he said nothing.

Good. This was humiliating enough.

"I'm glad you're here," Bree blurted. In her mind, when she'd pictured this moment, she had definitely not imagined Zacharias stood nearby with a shit-eating grin. But the embarrassment was worth it when Otis' face brightened, and a slow smile spread over his face.

"Me too," he said quietly, and it was like they were alone. Shivers skated over Bree's skin. After a long moment, a voice piped up at her elbow.

"You know, we've got this, boss. You don't have to hover."

It took Bree a second to realize Jason was talking to her—no one had ever called her boss—but when her frazzled mind caught up, she cleared her throat and nodded. He was right. They were busy here, and if she wasn't serving, she was in the way. Bree put all the work in planning tonight, and now she just had to let it unfold.

Her heeled boots wobbled as she stepped out from behind the bar. This was an outfit she'd never have considered before: smart ankle boots, black pants, and a cherry red blazer.

As soon as she'd tried it on though, she knew. This was it. She finally looked the part.

Out from behind the bar, Bree felt vulnerable. Everyone could see the whole of her, and she found herself hovering awkwardly against the wall. Claire dragged Zacharias off to play darts, and when Otis came to lean by her side, she could have wept from relief or nerves.

"I wasn't sure you'd come."

Otis shook his head, smiling down at his shoes. "I told you before, Bree. I'll always come. Always." On that last word, he looked up at her, his amber eyes bright and intense. Bree reached out without thinking, scrabbling for his hand, and when their fingers linked her heart ached in relief.

"I don't deserve that kind of devotion," she murmured. Otis opened his mouth to argue, but she held up her free hand. "No one does. But I'm selfishly glad that I have it."

"You do." His voice was fierce. Urgent. "And you deserve it, Bree."

She cast one last glance around the bar. Everything was going as planned. Oh, there were odd hiccups—the occasional shatter of glass; the harried expressions on her bartenders' faces—but it was nothing her staff couldn't handle. Nothing they hadn't planned for.

She was extraneous. A pair of watchful eyes, yes, but would it be so bad if she briefly looked away?

Bree found she didn't care. This bar was her baby, but

if something went wrong, she would handle it. Right now, there were things she needed to say to Otis Pascale. Privately. Without these drinkers gawping.

"Come with me." She tugged on his hand, and Otis pushed off the wall easily. "I'll give you the tour." His eyes sparked, but she could see the exact moment he reined in his hope. That he forced himself not to expect anything.

Well.

Bree would see about that.

Chapter 20

⚜

*O*tis wove through the Silver Bullet crowds, his fingers still wrapped around Bree's. Leaning over, he whispered in her ear as they dodged a huddle of laughing tourists.

"You know, the name of this place—Silver Bullet. In hindsight, that was kind of a red flag."

Bree smirked, her cheeks shifting as she stared straight forward. Otis watched the tiny movement, his heart pounding in his chest as she led him through the press of people to a door at the back of the room. It was nondescript, no doubt so as to avoid attention from the drinkers, and Otis was relieved to see Bree pull a key from around her neck and slide it into the lock.

Good. If he couldn't be close to her himself, at least she was taking precautions. Taking her safety seriously after the nightmare of a few months ago. Otis resisted the urge to praise her out loud and followed Bree up a narrow set of stairs.

This part of the building was clearly done up too, but with far less effort put into the decor. The walls were clean white, the steps well-cut oak, and they creaked under Otis' weight as he followed Bree up away from the bar.

It's her home, a voice whispered in his head. He knew she lived here now, of course—he wasn't a completely neglectful mate. But he never dared hope that he might see her private spaces. Hope churned in Otis' chest, knitting his rib cage tight, but he forced himself to follow in silence. Whatever Bree wanted from him, he would give without question. He'd sworn not to push.

"This, um. This is the bathroom." Bree nudged a door open once the stairs flattened into a narrow hallway. Otis peered into the small, shadowy space, his shifter's eyes picking out clean tiles and basic but well-maintained features.

"Very nice."

She scoffed. "Shut up."

Otis held up his hands. "You're right. It's hideous." The grin they shared made his heart squeeze in his chest, the pang almost painful. Then Bree turned away and he could breathe again, letting out a gust of air.

"This is the kitchen." It was the same story. Neat, clean and simple. To a casual eye, it might seem depressing, but Otis could see the love poured into every inch of this building. Yes, Bree's private rooms were modest, but she'd redone this building with her bare hands. He knew what that satisfaction felt like—he'd also spent the last few months elbow deep in sawdust and tins of paint. His cabin was almost completely rebuilt, sped along by the help of his pack.

Bree didn't have a pack. She'd done this all by herself. Tears of pride welled in Otis' eyes, and he blinked them away with a start.

"And this, um. This is my bedroom." They were at the

top of the building. When Otis followed Bree through the doorway, he had to stoop almost in half, and he craned his neck awkwardly to take in the space.

There was a double bed, low to the ground and haphazardly made. A colorful rug that he recognized from the emporium's clearance basket, and a squishy armchair next to a bookcase and coffee table. Bree watched him take in the room, her eyes glued to his face, but he didn't have to fake his smile.

"It's sweet. Homey."

Bree let out a breath. "Yeah."

They stood for a moment longer. Well, Bree stood, her head brushing against the ceiling. Otis stooped, his hands shoved awkwardly in his pockets.

"Well…" Otis didn't want to overstay his welcome. He jerked his thumb back at the doorway. "I'll clear out of your room." He'd barely begun to turn, shuffling around the cramped attic space, when Bree's arm shot out and grabbed his arm.

She held him lightly. Asking him to stay, but not insisting. That bubble of hope swelled in Otis' chest, until he was surprised he didn't burst like a balloon.

"Don't go," Bree whispered. "I mean, you know. Not if you don't want to." She smiled at him cautiously, and she looked so gods-damned nervous that Otis' heart nearly broke in two.

She was his mate. She never had to be nervous around him. Didn't she know that by now?

"I never want to go." It took some maneuvering, but Otis reached out and tucked a brown lock of hair behind her ear. "Never, Bree." He was barely done speaking when she launched forward, pressing her lips to his.

The first time Bree had kissed him, Otis had tried to commit it to memory. Her scent; the weight of her arms wrapped

Chapter 20

around his neck; the sensation of their mouths sliding together. He'd thought he'd got it all—the most important details—but this kiss proved what a fool he was.

There was no reproducing this. No storing it in his memory. Bree was urgent and overwhelming. She invaded his senses and yanked at his heartstrings; she moaned into his mouth and almost made him burst into flames right there. Otis swept her into his arms as much as the low ceiling would allow, walking them back toward her bed.

"Are you sure?" he asked, his mouth never leaving hers. A horrible thought occurred to him and he forced the words out, dread sliding through his gut. "This isn't just a hookup, is it? This is more?"

"It's more," Bree confirmed, nibbling on his lower lip. She dropped back onto the mattress, tugging him down until he crawled over her, propped up on straight arms. She looked so perfect below him, her hair splayed across the pillow and her body arching up to meet his. She slid a hand around his neck, pulling his face down and peppering kisses up his jaw. When she reached his ear, she whispered the words he'd longed to hear for so long.

"This is it, Otis. I'm ready."

* * *

Humans thought they knew what pressure was when they slept with a new partner for the first time. Oh, sure, they wanted to please the other person. They wanted to be Good In Bed. And maybe they already loved their partner, and this was like the most nerve-wrecking kind of audition.

Well, they should try bedding their fated mate. It was the

only first time that would ever truly matter.

"Tell me what you like," Otis murmured against Bree's neck, desperately trying to concentrate despite the feel of her soft body against his. "Tell me how you want me, Bree."

She bit her lip, and seemed to actually consider his question, thank the gods. Otis knew full well that Bree liked sex—that she was experienced, and no doubt had her own preferences. He didn't begrudge her them for a moment. On the contrary, he wanted the crib sheet. Bree Mendez 101: How to make her scream.

"Like this," she said at last. "Face to face. I want to see you."

Alright. That was easy. Otis dipped his head, nibbling her chin, and smirked as she whispered one more thing, her fingers trailing up his back.

"But... don't be gentle, Pascale. I'm not going to break. I can take you."

Oh, hell yeah.

He growled, catching hold of her wrists and pressing her hands against the headboard. She sighed into his mouth, squirming as he held both wrists in one hand and dragged his other palm down the center of her body. He savored every dip and curve of her; dipped his head to inhale deeply at her throat.

Then he undressed her slowly, torturing her, driving her out of her mind. He paused and licked and nibbled her skin with every button he undid. He dragged her shirt off her shoulders then kissed her wrists, thrilling at her racing pulse beneath the thin skin.

She wanted this. She wanted *him*, just as much as she said. Otis lunged forward, sucking a bruise into her throat, marking her for all to see. Not as a wolf marks his mate, but as a man marks his lover. When he pulled back, satisfaction thrummed through him at the sight of her flushed skin.

"Stop teasing," Bree gritted out, pressing her thighs together. Her forehead was damp with sweat; her cheeks were pink and her eyes bright. Otis grinned, flicking open the button of her jeans.

"So impatient."

When he finally peeled off the last of her clothes, Otis studied Bree like an artwork. Because that's what she was—crafted with the same perfection as a woman eternalized in statues and paintings. He cupped her breasts, running his flattened tongue over her nipples. He trailed his lips down to her belly button.

"Come on, you prick," Bree ground out, tugging at the back of his shirt. He pushed up, rocking back on his heels and shedding his clothes quickly, even as he gave her a taunting smile.

"Been thinking about this a while?" he asked casually, fully expecting a punch to the shoulder. Instead, her answer knocked the air from him.

"Forever. Get over here, Pascale."

Well, he couldn't deny her now. And when he explored her, he found her slick and ready. Bree hooked her legs around his hips, dragging him toward her, and told him: "I take the witches' potion. We're good. Now skip the foreplay."

Easing inside her was like nothing he'd imagined. His soul sang out and tears sprang to his eyes. Otis buried his face in Bree's hair as he pushed deeper—she'd never let him live it down if she saw him crying—and held his breath until they were sealed together.

"Finally," Bree gasped. He couldn't agree more. And when they moved together, Bree urging him on with her heels, he couldn't suppress his groan. He pushed inside his mate, drawing away to enter her again, and for the first time in his life everything was completely, utterly perfect.

His soul was at peace. His wolf growled its approval. And Bree moaned like she felt it too.

Without thinking, his mouth naturally drifted to the spot where her neck met her shoulder. The spot where all wolves claimed their mate with a bite, sealing their bond for the rest of their lives. Otis only noticed what he was doing when the tips of his canines dragged over her skin and Bree moaned louder, bucking harder against him.

Otis jerked back, flushing. That was a step too far—an eternal commitment between two souls. He had no right to ask that of her yet, but his body got caught up in the moment. For a moment, he lost his rhythm, distracted by what he'd nearly done, but his hips didn't stutter until Bree spoke.

"Do it. Claim me. I told you, Pascale, I'm ready."

Otis faltered, sweat beading on his forehead as every instinct screamed out at him to *do it.* To take her at her word and ask questions later. He shook his head, trying to clear it.

"That can't be undone." He slowed his hips, staring down at her. "Once I claim you, the bond is sealed."

"Good," Bree huffed. "We know what we want. Why mess around?"

His tongue prodded at the tip of his canine. Even in his human form, his teeth were sharp.

"It might hurt," he warned. Bree's sly smile made his muscles quake.

"Good."

Right. Well, then.

Otis began to move again, and they fell easily back into their rhythm. And when his mouth found that spot on her shoulder,

Bree sighed and raked her nails down his back.

It was the work of a moment. A small bite: the pinch and scrape of his teeth. Bree hissed, still moving against him, then they both shuddered to a halt as the bond snapped taut between them. He could feel it, the tie between him and Bree—he could feel her emotions broadcast down the line as clear as the radio's weather report.

He felt her desire. Her shy hopes.

And her gut-clenching, soul-shaking love for him.

Otis let out a frankly embarrassing noise, burying his face in the crook of Bree's neck as they finished. He savored the tightening of her body around him: the sounds she made as her legs shook. And he finally, finally let himself go, following her off the cliff.

They lay in a sweaty pile for a while. He stroked her shoulder; she scratched at his beard. Then, when their breathing had returned to normal and the sounds of the band echoing through the floorboards faded away, Bree sighed.

"I should get up. Go and handle the transfer. Put a playlist on."

Otis shrugged. "Jason can do it."

She rolled her eyes at him, pushing to sit upright, but there was no irritation there. Only love. Dazed, smirking, dazzled love.

Otis laid back, watching his mate gather her clothes and clean herself up enough to head back downstairs. Back down to the business she'd built from a wreckage; back to their friends and the laughing crowds and cool, crisp beers beaded with condensation.

Oh, yeah. Otis pushed himself up too, ready to follow.

This was the life.

Epilogue

❧

*L*aughter echoed across the desert wastes as Bree approached the cabin. It was typical of Otis: when faced with the trauma of his home burning down, he responded by rebuilding it exactly as it had been, but twenty feet further into the wilderness. The cabin still sat ass-backwards, with the porch steps and front door pointing away from the town towards the valley.

At some point last night, Zacharias and a few of the wolves sneaked out here and wrapped a giant red ribbon around the wooden cabin. Bree snorted when she saw it, elbowing Claire beside her.

"Is that supposed to wind Otis up? He'll love that shit."

Claire shrugged. "Zacharias is a secret sweetheart."

Bree wasn't so sure about that. She counted Zacharias among her close friends these days, and still would retch before calling the vamp a sweetheart.

"If you say so," Olivia said mildly from Bree's other side. Bree shot her a grin, and the librarian's glasses shifted as she raised her eyebrows.

She looked brighter today. Perkier than she had in months. Bree had nearly bitten through her tongue when she stopped by Olivia's apartment on the way over, she was so freaking excited to see her friend looking well.

She'd been worried. They all had. They were one more bad week away from an intervention.

"Have you seen inside?" Claire asked, scuffing her sneakers as she walked.

"Nope." Otis had been secretive as hell about this cabin. He'd insisted on rebuilding it from scratch, allowing only the help of his pack. Bree offered to help too once they were dating, but each time Otis shook his head with a mysterious smile, and said the cabin was her gift and she'd have to wait and see.

Screw that. If anyone else had told Bree that, she'd have already broken in before they were done talking.

But this was Otis, and he was so charmingly excited about his project... she hadn't wanted to ruin it. So here she was, trailing across the desert with half of the Boiling River locals in tow, ready for the grand reopening.

"It's your private cabin," she'd told him, exasperated. "Not the reopening of the Louvre."

Otis had beamed even wider, talking on like she'd never interrupted, promising booze and fireworks and the best barbecue for miles around.

The horizon glowed red, bleeding the dying rays of light over the mountains, then in the space of a few minutes, the sky darkened. This was planned, too: a night-time event, so that all of Boiling River's supernaturals could attend. Bree watched her feet as best she could, blinking through the gloom and thanking the gods that her boots had thick soles. You didn't wander in the desert at night with only a pair of sandals between your toes and the scorpions. Bree thought she heard something crunch beneath one boot, and cringed but walked on.

Nearly there. Then she could see what all the fuss was about.

Otis made good on his promises of food and festivities. The moment they stepped into the pool of warm lamplight surrounding the cabin, cold bottles of beer were thrust into their hands. The wolves milled around the crowd, handing out drinks and pointing out the groaning tables of food. Someone was playing guitar, picking quickly at the strings, and the barbecue crackled and popped as Otis manned the grill.

Bree slipped through the crowd, sliding her arms around his waist and pressing her nose between his shoulder blades. Immediately, the longing settled in her chest, and her nerves calmed. He was here. They were together again.

It had been less than twenty-four hours since she saw him last, but still the fierceness of the mating bond took Bree by surprise. Somehow, she managed to forget each time the gnawing sense of loss she felt after a few hours away from him. Then she'd leave Otis for the day—to go to work, or to see her friends—and the need to see him again would build and build until finally she made her excuses and slipped away.

This was exactly what she'd been afraid of. Being tied to another person, no longer free to make her own choices. But with Otis, it didn't bother her like she'd thought it would. It didn't feel like a prison sentence.

Nope. Bree finally understood how freaking lucky she was. "Are you hungry?"

Otis spoke without turning round, but the warmth that filled his voice was just for her. He balanced his tongs on the grill and ran his palms along her forearms, raising goosebumps in their wake.

"In some ways," Bree said lightly, stifling a smile at Otis' growl. "Too bad you need to entertain half the town."

He turned around in her arms, tucking her hair behind her ear. Bree smirked up at him, her heart rioting in her chest.

Otis bent and whispered: "Say the word. I'll start another fire."

Bree snorted. "If you knew me, you wouldn't tempt me like that."

"Oh, I know you." Otis' eyes sparked. "I know every inch of you, Bree Mendez, inside and out."

A throat cleared behind them, and Bree smiled sheepishly over her shoulder at Olivia. Her friend was pale in the lamplight, her white cheeks almost blue, and her icy blonde hair glittered like frost. Somehow, despite living in the desert, Olivia always contrived to seem cold. She wore knitted, draping jumpers and fluffy scarves. Woolen socks peeked out of her boots.

"What's up, Liv? You hungry?"

Olivia shook her head, then paused, as though building up to something. But finally, all she said was: "Can I show you something?"

She really should eat, Bree thought as she followed her friend away from the crowds around the side of the building. The scent of smoke followed them, along with the sounds of guitar strings and the chatter of their neighbors. Somewhere, back in the press of people, Mabel, the local banshee, let out a bloodcurdling scream. The guitar paused, and the chatter faded until Mabel's scream broke off in a throaty cough. Then the music started up again and the crowd laughed and talked, and

Bree's boots crunched as she followed Olivia into the darkness.

"Here." Olivia stopped at the back of the cabin, where moonlight washed the wood with a silvery glow.

"Um." Bree glanced at the building. The woodwork was solid, and the red ribbon was still tied in place. "It's nice, Liv."

Her friend huffed. "Not the cabin. There's something…" She trailed off, looking over her shoulder, then stepped closer to the building. Olivia put her face an inch from the dark window and breathed on the glass.

Her breath fogged. It clouded over the glass, staining it temporarily white, then faded away.

"Uh." Bree glanced over her shoulder, worried. Had Olivia snapped? Did she need to find Claire?

"No, it's—" Olivia broke off with a huff. Then she turned and spoke to the empty air, her voice sharp and annoyed. "Are we doing this or not? Because it's not my problem."

Bree stared, speechless, as Olivia leaned back to the window, fogging it with her breath once again.

"There," she said, victorious, stabbing her finger at the glass. Bree followed where she was pointing, then jerked back.

As she watched, an invisible finger traced a word into the steamed up glass. *S…O…S.*

"I'm not insane," Olivia blurted. She pointed at the word again, her finger shaking. "I'm haunted."

THE END

Want more from Boiling River? Have you read the FREE bonus story about Olivia's mysterious admirer? Claim your copy of *Static Noise* here: https://BookHip.com/PKKRSH

Epilogue

And be sure to check out the next book in the Supernatural Airwaves series: *Ghost Track*. Read on for a sneak preview…

Teaser: Ghost Track

Starlight Springs was built on a ledge halfway up the valley wall. It clung to the rock face, an odd cluster of lights that shone across the wastes at night. On a Sunday morning, though, the retreat bustled with energy, and Bree circled the makeshift parking lot three times before finding a space. Olivia lurched gratefully out of the truck, pointedly avoiding looking back at the steep, narrow road.

She'd forgotten that part. As teenagers, it barely registered with her that they were driving up a tightrope of a mountain path. She'd been so cocky, so filled with the hubris of adolescence, that it hadn't even occurred to her that they were inches from a terrible fall.

It occurred to her now, alright. Where had that fearless girl gone?

"Let's go," she muttered, gripping her rolled paper with damp hands, and Bree and Claire fell into step behind her. Starlight Springs loomed ahead, a sprawling adobe palace with candles burning on every spare windowsill. Ivy and other climbing plants tumbled down the walls, and mosaic tiles were inlaid in the stone, depicting local gods and ancient warriors. The heady smell of incense hung in the air, and somewhere nearby, running water burbled.

Harp music lulled them as they marched up the front path, interrupted by someone barking orders inside. As Olivia stepped into the lobby, squinting against the sudden gloom, she found a curvy, harried woman stood beside the reception desk, a basket of laundry propped on one hip. Her wild, dark curls were piled on her head, and a few had escaped to dangle over her shoulders.

The woman stopped yelling up the stairs and pasted on a bright smile.

"Hello," she said, voice suddenly serene. "Welcome. Come inside."

"Um." Bree elbowed Olivia in the back, and she stumbled forward, approaching the desk. The paper crinkled in her grip as she held it out to the woman. "Are you a witch?"

Some of the manufactured calm slid off the woman's face, and her canny eyes fixed on the paper.

"I am. Are you a paying guest?"

Bree snorted and elbowed past. She dug her wallet out of her back pocket as she walked, slapping a handful of bills down on the counter. "Three day passes," she told the pink-haired receptionist. The girl—she barely looked their age—jumped and nodded, plucking up the bills with shaky fingers.

Olivia swallowed and forced a smile onto her face. She held the paper out higher.

"Delilah." The witch tugged the paper from her grip, setting her laundry basket down on the marble floor with a thump. "Sun witch."

"Um, th-thank you. Olivia. Librarian."

The smirk the witch shot her was friendlier this time, but

it faded to a frown as she rolled out the paper. She traced her fingertips over the ghost's splotchy letters. She held the paper up to the sunlight filtering through the tall windows. Then Delilah hummed and began to pace, marching back and forth in the lobby.

Olivia backed up to the reception desk, ignoring the hushed murmurs behind her as the receptionist issued three toweled robes and day passes. She watched the witch—Delilah—pace up and down, her fingers curling into tight fists.

"Relax," Claire murmured, making Olivia jump. She nudged her with her shoulder, her freckled face open and warm. "We're in the right place."

Olivia nodded, swallowing down the lump in her throat. She leaned closer to whisper back.

"I feel like I'm in trouble at school."

Claire snorted, the sound echoing around the lobby, and Delilah turned on her heel and strode over.

"What is this?" She thrust the paper toward Olivia, raising a stern eyebrow. "Is this a prank?"

Olivia shook her head, crossing her arms. She wasn't taking back that paper until she had some answers.

"I'm being haunted." She launched into an account of the last few months—the voice she'd heard on the radio; the notes on the mirror; the message. And all while she spoke, Delilah scowled down at the paper like it had personally offended her.

"A ghost didn't write this," the witch snapped, like she'd caught them in a lie. Olivia shrugged helplessly.

"Well, *something* did."

Delilah grunted and took up pacing once more, pausing halfway across the tiles to yell at the chandelier.

"Luke! I need you!"

A handsome, dangerous-looking man materialized at the top of the stairs. He strolled down the steps, a graceful hand resting on the banister, his fluid gait and black tunic reminiscent of a panther.

"You bellowed, my darling?"

"Look at this." Delilah thrust the paper into his chest. The man smoothed it out, a thoughtful expression settling over his sharp features. "One of yours?"

He shook his head, mouth twisting to one side.

"I rather think not."

"One of… what?" Olivia asked, her voice timid in the cool lobby. She cleared her throat, straightening her shoulders. She wasn't afraid, damn it, and she didn't need to sneak around like a mouse. Olivia raised her chin. "What do you mean, 'one of yours'?"

"Souls," the man said casually, tossing the word at her over his shoulder. He turned back to the paper, tracing the words with his thumb. "Damned souls."

Olivia barely had time to mull that over before the man handed the paper back to Delilah with a shrug.

"This is not the work of a soul. I'm sorry, my love."

Delilah dismissed the man with a wave of her hand, and he winked at Olivia as he sauntered back out of the lobby. She rocked back on her heels, the reception desk digging into her spine, and when the witch said nothing for a full minute, she tossed her hands in the air.

"If he's not a ghost or a soul, what else could he—"

"I don't know." Delilah cocked her head, a faint smile tugging her plump lips. "How intriguing." She smacked the paper, the sound making Olivia jump, then gave her a grin. "Enjoy your day at the spa, my dear. Leave this with me."

* * *

He was a loose swarm of atoms floating in Olivia's kitchen near the bread bin when footsteps bounded up the stairs outside. The key scraped into the lock, the door handle rattling impatiently, and muffled voices hissed at each other through the door.

Interesting. Olivia rarely had visitors.

He pulled himself together by sheer force of will, gathering the remembered pieces of himself one atom at a time. It was harder when she was not around. Her presence anchored him somehow, made him stronger. More resolute. With Olivia on the other side of the door, he had only the fuzzy memories of who he used to be to hold himself intact.

The voices outside the door grew louder, and he sighed as he stood once more on the kitchen tiles. His bare toes grew chilled against the cold floor, and his swim shorts whispered against his skin as he strode into the living room, to the relative warmth of the rug.

"Hello?" The door burst open, spilling three women into the small apartment. It never felt cramped here when it was just Olivia and him—for starters, he could meld with the furniture if he needed to—but with three grown bodies stomping around, the rooms seemed more cluttered than before. He moved to stand in the middle of the coffee table, watching them swirl around him.

One woman with wild dark hair threw herself bodily onto the squat, plump sofa, scuffing it over the floorboards.

Olivia winced. The others didn't notice, but he did. He noticed everything about her.

"Are you here?" the redhead called, hands planted on her

hips by the bookcase. She stared into the corners of the living room, like she might find him there floating in a bed sheet.

"Yes," he told her pointlessly. He always answered. They never heard.

"He's here," Olivia murmured, and his eyebrows shot up his forehead. She could tell when he was near? Could she smell him, hear him, *feel* him?

But no. She peered into another corner of the room, at the squishy armchair she loved to curl up in to read.

"I missed you." He watched Olivia shoo the brunette off the sofa, the two of them pushing it up against the wall. "I slipped into nothing again." The redhead grabbed one end of the coffee table, dragging it through his legs to the other side of the room, rucking up great folds in the rug as she went. "She won't like that," he told the interloper, jerking his head at Olivia. "She likes things neat."

Sure enough, Olivia darted across the room, kneeling to yank the creases out of the rug. She flipped it back instead, over the top of the coffee table, then the three women stood together and stared at the floorboards. Their chests rose and fell in unison, their cheeks flushed from their redecorating, and a long moment stretched out before the brunette broke the silence.

"So." She dug out her phone, showing the others the screen. "I googled it. This is a pentagram."

"Is there a special way of drawing it?" the redhead mused, cocking her head. "Or do I just copy the image?" Both heads swung toward Olivia.

She pulled out several folded sheets of paper from the pocket of her pinafore dress, smoothing the creases with trembling fingers. He wanted to go to her, to soothe those nerves, but

163

something held him back.

A pentagram. For him.

This could be a good thing. It could be his lucky break. Or his librarian might have finally grown sick of him.

"This is to help me, right?" he called to her, rubbing a palm over his chest. The memory of his heart slammed against his rib cage. "This isn't pest control?"

Because he was a pest. No doubt about it. He'd dogged her every waking minute for months until she'd finally accepted he was real. He'd kept her awake; he'd moved things around; on one especially strong night, he'd flooded her bathroom.

He wasn't proud. He was desperate. No one else had come close to hearing him in Boiling River. To sensing his existence. Only Olivia heard his desperate pleas on the radio, recorded over the town's local jingles. Only *her* head twitched in his direction sometimes.

"It doesn't say." Olivia turned the paper over, scanning the back. She pushed her glasses up her nose, frowning at the lines of curly handwriting looping over the paper. "It just says draw the pentagram. Then burn the herbs, light the candles, and say the words."

"Right." The redhead clapped her hands together, dropping to her knees. She rummaged in a satchel, producing a piece of white chalk, and crawled to the center of the floorboards. "That's my cue."

* * *

He'd never seen magic done before. Not *real* magic, with a spell gifted by an actual witch. Sure, back when he had a body and a life, he watched videos online and even went to a magic show once as a kid. He'd traveled through Boiling River on his way… somewhere… and haunted the town since, and you couldn't spend five minutes in Boiling River without seeing something supernatural.

This, though. This was different.

It was occult. Mysterious. Kind of freaky.

"And you're definitely not exorcising me?" he asked Olivia for the third time as he trailed after her around the apartment. It was impossibly more crowded than before, with two men and a woman joining midway through the preparations. One man—a pale vampire with long dark hair—lounged against the wall and watched the backside of the bent over redhead with shameless appreciation. The other, a large black man with startling amber eyes, was sniffing around the kitchen counter as the brunette ground herbs with a mortar and pestle.

"It smells like a pizzeria," the man groaned, dipping his face to sniff at the bowl. He dug his phone out of his back pocket, shaking his head. "I can't do it. I'm gonna order."

Whatever was about to happen with the pentagram, it was turning into a sideshow. Olivia's neat, prim apartment was crammed with bodies; beers were cracked open and somewhere music was playing. The new woman who'd joined—a short, plump woman with a glossy black bob—sat cross-legged in Olivia's armchair, gnawing on a chocolate bar.

He wanted to shoo them all out. He wanted to pick up their mess, put the furniture back, and smooth the worried crease from Olivia's forehead. She watched the proceedings with her teeth buried in her lip, consulting her sheets of paper endlessly and blinking owlishly around the room from behind her glasses.

"I'll be better," he swore, trying and failing to pluck at

her sleeve. His fingers passed straight through the material, through the heat of her arm. "I won't touch the faucets again. Send them away, sweetheart."

This was his home now. The only place he'd felt any smidgen of peace since waking up without his body in the town square. And maybe this spell was to help him or hurt him, but either way, he wanted these people gone.

They were messing up Olivia's stuff. Invading her perfectly organized space. And though she smiled at them, chatting and laughing, he could read the strain in her eyes.

"Go on." He crossed to the vampire, flicking at a long dark lock of hair which had escaped from its tie. The hairs twitched, but the vampire didn't notice. "Get out of here. She's tired, can't you see?"

The vampire lifted a bottle of blood to his lips, his eyes fixed on the artist knelt on the floor.

"Okay." Olivia cleared her throat, her voice strong as it carried through the room. He remembered the first time he'd heard her read to the children in the library—how surprised he'd been that buried in this quiet, reserved girl, there was a deep well of self-assurance.

No one here was surprised, though. They fell quiet, turning to watch her expectantly.

Olivia stood beside the pentagram, nudging a lit candle closer to a point with the toe of her ankle boot. She called out a checklist—*candles ready, pentagram ready, herbs ready*—then straightened her shoulders and closed her eyes. When she spoke, her voice was gentle. Almost tender.

"Alright. You need to stand in the pentagram."

It took a moment for him to realize that she was speaking to him. He jerked, stepping back automatically and merging with a lampshade.

"Are you in there?"

"No," he said, voice hoarse. It didn't matter. She couldn't hear him. And so she began to speak, reading from the paper, trusting so absolutely that he'd do as she asked. He lunged forward before she reached the end of the first line, panic clawing at his throat, and skidded to a halt in the center of the chalked floorboards. The candles flared around him, their flames shooting towards the ceiling, and the woman in the armchair sucked in a gasp.

"It's working," the amber-eyed man muttered in the kitchen. The brunette nodded, elbowing him in the ribs.

The words were ancient. Lost words with hidden meanings, their secrets known only to the witches. Olivia squinted as she read them, holding the paper inches from her nose, but whatever the words meant, each landed on him like a blow.

His feet anchored to the floorboards, fusing him in place.

His head snapped back on his neck, his eyes glowing at the ceiling.

And his arms were yanked to the sides, almost tearing from their sockets.

He cried out, begging Olivia to stop, but his mouth made no sound. Pins and needles filled him, starting at the soles of his bare feet and surging up, through his legs and torso and skull, stabbing thousands of tiny points into his faint flesh. Numbness rushed through him in waves, and each time the prickling came back harder, the sensation slicing through to his core. Static crackled through his ears, darkness filled his eyes, and when the pain finally faded, his ears were ringing.

He looked around, chest heaving, sweat slicking his skin.

Six pairs of eyes stared back.

And one pair in particular—icy blue, behind thick-framed glasses—widened as they saw him for the first time. He raised a hand, his limb almost unbearably heavy, and waved.

"Um. Hi."

Check out Ghost Track here: https://books2read.com/ghosttrack

About the Author

Tabby Monroe writes quirky & creepy paranormal romance.

When she's not writing, Tabby can be found baking, hiking, and befriending local cats.

She lives on the Welsh coast with her very own gorgeous vamp.

You can connect with me on:
- https://www.tabbymonroe.com
- https://www.bookbub.com/authors/tabby-monroe
- https://www.amazon.com/~/e/B08PDKSHB1

Subscribe to my newsletter:
- https://www.tabbymonroe.com/newsletter